U0019890

九歌文庫936

Learning English From Uncle Lee : Good Fate

跟李伯伯學英文 2
Good Fate

李家同　著
康士林·鮑端磊　譯

目　錄

讀 者
A Reader

鮑端磊　譯

　　我去看李家同，就是為了要解答我的一個疑問，這小子變了沒有？現在我終於得到答案了，雖然我已認不出來他，他還是沒有變。

　　I went to see Lee Chia-tung to find an answer to a question. Had I changed? Now I finally had my answer. Although I did not recognize him, he hadn't changed at all.

我

是李家同的忠實讀者。

我一直是一個工人，幾年前退休了，我因此常去圖書館借書看，就這樣無意中發現了李家同這個作者。我之所以喜歡看他的文章，多多少少是因為他常替我們這種社會上的弱勢團體講話。自從看了他的書以後，我發現他常常在《聯合報》副刊上寫文章。有一天，我讀到他關於紫外線的文章，紫外線也許真的有害於人體，但是像我們這種人，一輩子在大太陽下工作，為什麼從來沒有人關心過我們？

---

loyal（adj.）忠實的
worker（n.）工人、勞動者
retire（v.）退休
library（n.）圖書館
borrow（v.）借、借入
haphazard（adj.）偶然的、無意中

discovery（n.）發現
author（n.）作者
essay（n.）散文、文章
pretty much 大致上、幾乎
seem to 好像、似乎

I am a loyal reader of Lee Chia-tung.

I had always been a worker. I retired several years ago, and that's when I began to go to the library to borrow books. That's how I made thc haphazard discovery of this author by the name of Lee Chia-tung. The reason I had always liked reading his essays was that in pretty much all he wrote, he seemed to talk for people in society who were vulnerable like me in one way or the other. From the time I began reading his writings, I discovered he was doing columns for the United Daily News. One day I saw how he even wrote about ultraviolet rays. Maybe ultraviolet rays really could hurt people's health. But for someone like me who had worked his entire life in the sun, well, why was it that no one showed any particular concern for us?

---

vulnerable（adj.）脆弱、易受傷害的　　hurt（v.）傷害
writing（n.）著作、作品　　health（n.）健康
discover（v.）發現　　entire life（n.）一生、一輩子
column（n.）專欄　　particular（adj.）特別的
ultraviolet rays（n.）紫外線　　concern（n.）關心、關懷

　　我對李家同開始有了好奇心，他長得什麼樣子呢？有一天，我和一位圖書館館員談天，他告訴我李家同這個傢伙話多得很，惟恐沒有人和他聊天。他鼓勵我去看他，他也幫我查到了靜宜大學的電話。我打電話去靜宜大學，被轉到了校長室，他的秘書立刻替我約了一個時間。

　　李家同果真是個健談的人，我問他有關他書裡的文章，他都很快樂地回答。我看他很喜歡和讀者來往，大概有讀者造訪，作者的虛榮心就可以滿足吧。

---

increasingly（adv.）日益、越來越多
curious（adj.）好奇的
official（n.）館員、公務員
fellow（n.）人、傢伙
fear（n.）害怕、恐懼
encourage（v.）鼓勵

look up 查找
dial（v.）打電話、撥打
transfer（v.）轉移、轉接
secretary（n.）祕書
right away 馬上、立刻
arrange（v.）安排

I began to get increasingly curious about Lee Chia-tung. What did he look like? I got to talking with an official at the library, and he told me this Lee fellow was a man of many words. It seemed his only fear was not having someone to talk to. He encouraged me to go see him. He helped me look up the telephone number for Providence University. I dialed that number for Providence and got transferred to the president's office. His secretary right away arranged an appointment for me.

Well, Lee Chia-tung really was an easy man to talk with. I asked him about some things in those pages in his books, and he answered my questions happily enough. I saw he enjoyed relating directly with readers. It's probably true that visits by readers satisfy a writer's natural sense of vanity.

appointment（n.）約會、會面
happily（adv.）快樂地、開心地
enjoy（v.）喜愛、享受
relate（v.）相處
directly（adv.）直接、坦率

probably（adv.）也許、大概
visit（n.）拜訪、造訪
satisfy（v.）滿足
sense of vanity（n.）虛榮心

在我們交談的時候，不停地有人進來，好像都是學校裡的什麼長，我沒有進過大學，弄不清楚這些頭銜。有一位顯然是學生，進來討論一個學問上的問題，我更聽不懂。電話鈴響了，李家同去接電話，這次談話特別長，我就站起來看那些照片。李家同辦公室的書架上以及矮櫃上放滿了照片，除了一張他自己的全家福以外，全部都是年輕人的照片，也有不少是穿軍裝的照片，大概都是學生做預官時的照片。

regular（adj.）經常的
a stream of（n.）一連串、一系列
various（adj.）不同的、許多
university（n.）大學
department（n.）科系
unit（n.）單位
manage to 設法做到、成功做到
highfalutin（adj.）誇張的
folk（n.）人、成員
title（n.）職稱、頭銜
straight（adj.）正確的
obviously（adv.）明顯、顯然

While we were talking, a regular stream of people kept coming in. They all seemed to be officials of various university departments or units. I myself never managed to make it into a university. I couldn't keep all those highfalutin folks and their titles straight.

One of them was obviously a student. He came to discuss some kind of scholarly question. I couldn't understand a thing they were saying. One time when the telephone rang and Lee Chia-tung took the call, he stayed on the line particularly long. I got to my feet and looked at his photographs. The bookcases and cabinets in Lee's office were well stocked with picture frames. With the exception of one photo, a portrait of his whole family, the pictures were all of young people. Quite a few were of people in military uniforms. They probably were pictures of students who had served in the military

---

discuss（v.）討論
scholarly（adj.）學問的
understand（v.）了解、明白
photograph（n.）照片
bookcase（n.）書架
cabinet（n.）櫥櫃

stock（v.）貯存
picture frame（n.）相框
exception（n.）例外
portrait（n.）相片、人像
military uniform（n.）軍服
serve（v.）服役

　　有一張照片，是一大堆年輕人穿軍裝的照片，大概
他們才受階，我在這麼多人中間，一眼就認出了李家
同。當然囉，他完全變了。也難怪，他現在已經六十
歲，那時候只有二十二歲，四十年過去，任何人都變老
了。可是我依然將他認了出來。李家同發現我居然認出
了他年輕時的照片，大為驚訝。他說他這麼多的訪客
中，從來沒有能夠認得出他在這張照片中，每次指給學
生看，學生都說怎麼變得這麼厲害，只有一個會拍馬屁
的學生說，簡直沒有變，事後被他罵了一頓，不能如此
口是心非也。

---

reserve officer（n.）預官
dress（v.）穿衣
promote（v.）晉升
midst（n.）中間、中央
bunch（n.）群、夥

spot（v.）認出、發現
completely（adv.）完全、徹底
no wonder 難怪
zoom（v.）畫面推近或拉遠

as reserve officers.

He had one picture in which everyone was young and dressed in military uniforms. They had probably all just gotten promoted. There in the midst of the whole bunch of them my eye spotted Lee Chia-tung. Oh, of course, he had changed completely. And no wonder! He was 60 years old now. He was only 22 back then. Forty years had zoomed by and everybody changes when that happens. But I still picked him out.

Lee Chia-tung was surprised when he found out I had recognized him as a young fellow. He said that lots of guests had dropped by over the years, but no one had ever picked him out in that picture. Every time he pointed out the picture to students, why, the students all said, "How could someone change so much?" There was only one student—a real brown noser—who claimed he hadn't

pick out 辨認出
find out 發現
recognize（v.）認得、認出
fellow（n.）人、傢伙

drop by 順便拜訪
point out 指出
brown noser（n.）拍馬屁的人
claim（v.）聲稱

　　我問〈車票〉是不是真的故事，他說是虛構的。他

說〈我的媽媽來看我〉是真的。我看過〈我的媽媽來看

我〉，當時也很感動，故事有關新店軍人監獄的一位受

刑人，他老是幻想他的媽媽去看他，其實他的家人一直

和他斷絕了關係，從來沒有人去看他。李家同不知情，

去他家拜訪他的母親，也就在無意中促成了家人的團

圓。這位受刑人後來就有媽媽去看他了。

---

a bit 一點

ridiculous（adj.）可笑的、荒謬的

fabricate（v.）虛構、杜撰

move（v.）感動、打動

soldier（n.）士兵、軍人

actually（adv.）其實、實際上

changed a bit. After talking like that, he got told off by Lee Chia-tung. You couldn't tell such a ridiculous lie and get away with it.

I asked him if "The Ticket" was a real story, and he told me it was fabricated. He said "My Mother Came to See Me" was real. I had read "My Mother Came to See Me." At the time, it moved me. It was a story about a soldier who landed himself in a military prison in Xindian. He was always imagining his mother would come to visit him. Actually, the guy's family had cut all ties with him. Not a single relative ever came to visit him. Lee Chia-tung didn't know anything about the situation, and he went to see the prisoner's mother. Without realizing what he was doing, he brought that family together again. Later that prisoner did get that visit from his mother.

---

cut all ties 斷絕關係、切斷所有聯繫　　realize（v.）了解、意識到
relative（n.）親戚、家屬　　　　　　later（adv.）後來、以後
prisoner（n.）囚犯、受刑人

　　我問李家同那位受刑人有沒有和他聯絡過，他說沒有，他也不知道是什麼原因。我告訴他我也曾經在新店住過，知道那所軍人監獄在哪裡。

　　我們還談了不少有關他寫文章的動機。最後，他問我怎麼來的，我說我坐火車經由海線到沙鹿，他就請他的司機開車送我去沙鹿火車站，司機是一位胖胖的年輕人，脾氣非常好。

　　上了火車，我幾乎要崩潰了，我沒有想到他變得這麼老。我就是那位受刑人，當年他來看我，那麼年輕，頭髮全是黑的，現在已是半白，我還記得他穿軍裝的樣

---

happen（v.）發生
motivation（n.）誘因、動機
coast（n.）海岸、沿海

chauffer（n.）司機
heavy-set（adj.）胖的、粗壯的
good humored（adj.）心情愉快

I asked Lee Chia-tung if the prisoner ever got back in touch with him. He said no, that had never happened. He had no idea why. I told him I once lived in Xindian and knew where the military prison was. We talked quite a bit about his motivation for writing.

He finally asked how I had come. I said I'd taken the train along the coast to Shalu. He asked his chauffer to drive me to Shalu. The chauffer was a heavy-set young fellow, very good humored.

By the time I sat down on the train, I was ready to collapse. I had certainly never imagined he would look so old. I was that prisoner. When Lee Chia-tung came to see me back then, he was so young his hair was totally black. Now it was half white. I could still remember

的、脾氣好的　　　　　　　　imagine（v.）想像、猜想
collapse（v.）崩潰　　　　　totally（adv.）完全
certainly（adv.）當然

子，冬季服是藍的，夏季服是黃的。他退伍以後，立刻就要去美國，在退伍以前，來和我道別，我們雖然見面，卻不能握手，因為見面仍有一牆之隔，我記得他臨走前，拿起了軍帽戴上，立正向我敬了一個禮。我是一個小兵，少尉雖然是最低階的軍官，但也是軍官，軍官是不可以向小兵敬禮的，何況我還是個受刑人。我被他這個調皮的動作嚇了一跳，可是我記得他戴軍帽的樣子，滿神氣的。現在呢？我想他如果上公共汽車，一定會有人讓位子給他。

civilian（n.）平民百姓
army（n.）軍隊
shake hands 握手
separate（v.）分隔、分開
recall（v.）回想、憶起

salute（v.）敬禮
rank（n.）軍階、階級
private（n.）士兵
although（conj.）雖然、儘管
second lieutenant（n.）少尉

how he looked in his military uniform. He wore green in the winter and brown in the summer. When he became a civilian again, he quickly went to the United States. Before he got out of the army, he came to say goodbye to me. Although we saw each other, we could not shake hands, because a window separated us. I recalled how just before he left me, he took the hat off his head and saluted me. My rank was private, and although a second lieutenant was the lowest ranking officer, he was still an officer, and an officer was not supposed to salute a buck private. And on top of that, there I was—a prisoner. I was startled by his mischievous gesture. But I sure could remember how he wore that hat. He had looked like a god to me. And now? I thought if he ever climbed onto a bus, someone would jump up and offer him their seat.

---

officer（n.）軍官
be supposed to 應該、可以
buck private（n.）小兵、列兵
on top of that 此外、更何況
startle（v.）驚嚇、嚇一跳

mischievous（adj.）調皮的、淘氣的
gesture（n.）舉動、動作
climb（v.）登上
jump up 跳起來
offer（v.）提供、讓出

　　我感到非常難過，他變得如此之老。因為我的記憶中，只有他年輕時的樣子，我其實早該有此心理準備的，四十年了，我們都變了，我只知道我自己變了一個人，所以他完全認不出我，沒有想到的是，我也完全認不出他了。為什麼我不表明我的身分？理由很簡單，我不願意再談我的一生！大家都知道受刑人在監獄中很苦，很少人知道，出了監獄，在社會上討生活，他們會遭遇到多少困難？這種烙印所帶來的後遺症，李家同是不可能了解的，從他的小說中，不難看出這一點，他的小說中從未談過受刑人恢復自由以後的事。

　　當然，如果他認出了我，我會表明我是誰。可是，

---

sadness（n.）悲傷、難過　　　　reason（n.）原因、理由
memory（n.）回憶、記憶　　　　simple（adj.）簡單
prepare（v.）準備好　　　　　　suffer（v.）痛苦、受苦
mentally（adv.）心理上　　　　　ex-con（n.）前科犯、出獄犯人

Sadness was all I felt. How could he have become so old? All my memories of him were when he was young. I knew I should have prepared myself mentally. Forty years, well, we all change. I knew I had changed during that time too, and so he didn't recognize me at all. What I had never realized was I couldn't recognize him either. Why didn't I tell him who I was? The reason was simple. I didn't want to talk about my life. Everyone knows people in prison suffer, but why are there so few who see that after they come out, ex-cons meet all kinds of difficulties in adjusting to society? A brand on a man like that is a side-effect you carry with you your whole life through. Lee Chia-tung could never know what it was like. It wasn't hard to find that in his writings. He had never done stories about what it is like for prisoners after they get their freedom back.

Of course, had he recognized me, I'd have revealed

---

difficulty（n.）困難、困境
adjust to 適應
brand（n.）烙印、污名
side-effect（n.）後遺症、副作用

hard（adj.）困難的
freedom（n.）自由
reveal（v.）揭露、表明

他顯然沒有認出我來，我甚至帶了一本他寫的書給他簽名，他問了我的名字，我據實以告，他在書上寫了我的名字，可是一點表情也沒有。

我感到很疲倦，老年人，有時不該想到往事的；尤其像我這種人，更不該自討苦吃地去回憶往事。我要好好地睡一下，我累了。

一覺醒來，火車已快進台北車站，我忽然想起，當我認出李家同的時候，他應該已經猜到我是誰了，又有誰能夠認出他年輕時的樣子呢？他沒有問我為何能認出他，顯然是因為他知道我不願意表明我的身分，他尊重我想法，所以就不點出了。

---

autograph（v.）簽名
truth（n.）真相、事實
blank（n.）無表情、空白

exhausted（adj.）疲倦的
dwell（v.）回憶、停滯於（某種狀態）、活在（過去…等等）

who I was. But he obviously had not recognized me. I even brought one of his books for him to autograph for me. He asked me for my name, and I told him the truth. He wrote my name into my book, but his face was a blank

I felt exhausted. Once you become old, sometimes you shouldn't dwell on the past. That is especially true for a fellow like me. The thing not to do was beg for more pain and kill myself with old memories. I wanted to fall asleep. Oh, I felt tired.

Then it dawned on me. The train was just pulling into Taipei station, and I suddenly realized that when I recognized Lee Chia-tung, he should have been able to guess who I was. Who else would have been able to pick him out as a young man? He never asked me how I could know that was him. Clearly it was because he knew I didn't want to tell him who I was. He had

---

beg（v.）乞討
fall asleep 入睡、睡著
dawn on：使（某人）想到

pull into 進入、開進
guess（v.）猜出
clearly（adv.）顯然

　　我後來又說我在新店住過，也知道軍人監獄在哪裡，他仍然沒有問我在新店時做什麼的。那時候，他一定非常確定我是誰了。他向我道別的時候，曾對我揮手致意，揮手的姿勢像極了軍人敬禮，我給了他暗示我早就認識他了，他也回敬了一個暗示，他不僅也認出了我，而且還記得我們上次道別時的情境。

　　我去看李家同，就是為了要解答我的一個疑問，這小子變了沒有？現在我終於得到答案了，雖然我已認不出來他，他還是沒有變。

——原載八十八年五月五日《聯合副刊》

---

respect（v.）尊重　　　　　　slightest（adj.）最輕微的
locate（v.）位在　　　　　　 doubt（n.）懷疑
living（n.）生計、生活　　　　farewell（n.）道別、告別

respected my way, so he didn't show anything.

Then I said I had lived in Xindian, that I knew where that military prison was located. And still he didn't ask what I did for a living in Xindian. At that moment he must have known without the slightest doubt who I was. When he said farewell to me in his office, he had lifted his hand to his forehead, and the gesture was a soldier's salute. I had hinted to him that I knew him earlier in life, and he had hinted back. Not only had he recognized me. He still remembered the scene of our last farewell.

I went to see Lee Chia-tung to find an answer to a question. Had I changed? Now I finally had my answer. Although I did not recognize him, he hadn't changed at all.

---

lift（v.）舉起
forehead（n.）前額、額頭
hint（v.）暗示

earlier（adv.）早先、更早
scene（n.）景象、情境

如果米開朗基羅復活了
If Michelangelo were to be Born Again

康士林　譯

　　我的心又飛到加爾各答的「垂死之家」，這是德蕾莎修女為窮人所準備的地方，這裡看不到任何建築之美，可是在這裡，我可以感到人類最善良的一面。我永遠記得那些好心義工們握住垂死窮人手的畫面，這才是最美麗的畫面。

　　My heart had turned to Calcutta's "Home for the Dying," a place Mother Teresa had prepared for poor people. There is no architectural beauty there, but there I can feel the best goodness of people. I will forever remember the pictures of those good-hearted volunteers holding poor people on the verge of death. These are the most beautiful pictures.

我到靜宜去做校長以後，經常晚上不能回家吃晚飯，於是我就常去我的學生家混晚飯吃，常被我騷擾的是王嘉政。我喜歡到他家去要飯吃有很多原因，一來是他太太燒飯手藝很好；二來是他很會攝影，每次去必定會看到他的最新傑作；三來是他有一個聰明而可愛的兒子。

王嘉政在一家大哥大公司做事，他常常要出國去和外國的大哥大公司簽訂「漫遊」條約，每次簽約以後，就在當地的名勝或風景區遊玩。因為他的攝影技巧非常好，他每次拍的照片都有值得展覽的佳作，我每次去，都會欣賞一下他所拍的照片。

President（n.）校長、總統
frequently（adv.）經常、常常
bum（v.）討、乞討
supper（n.）晚餐
excellent（adj.）出色的、優秀的

photography（n.）攝影、照相
inevitably（adv.）必定、必然地
mobile phone（n.）手機、大哥大、行動電話
go abroad 出國

After I became the President of Providence University, I often was not able to return home for supper, so I frequently went to my students' home to bum a supper; and the one most often bothered by me was Wang Jiazheng. There were many reasons why I liked to go to his house for supper. First of all, his wife was an excellent cook; then, he was good at photography, so each time I went I would inevitably see his latest work. Finally, he had a smart, lovable son.

Wang worked at a mobile phone company and often had to go abroad to sign "roaming" contracts with foreign mobile phone companies. After the contract was signed, each time he would go sightseeing to a famous landmark or some special scenery. Because his skill at photography was extraordinary, his photographs were worth putting on exhibition. Every time I went to his

---

roaming（n.）漫遊
foreign（adj.）外國的
sightseeing（n.）觀光、遊覽
landmark（n.）地標、名勝
scenery（n.）風景、景色

skill（n.）技術、技藝
extraordinary（adj.）非凡的、傑出的
exhibition（n.）展覽、展示會

　　王嘉政顯然是一個唯美主義者，他的照片一概美得不得了，無論是人物，或是風景，都給我們一種美感，王嘉政的照片裡，找不到不美的東西。舉例來說，王嘉政所拍的人物中，好像沒有髮蒼蒼而齒牙動搖的老人。

　　王嘉政對他小兒子的教育，有他的一套。他希望他兒子有足夠的想像力，因此他不給兒子買太多太像真東西的玩具。他常鼓勵他兒子隨便拿一個物體，然後將這個物體想像成一件特別的東西，有時我看到他兒子在玩一根棍子，可是他一口咬定這是太空船，他說未來的太

obvious（adj.）顯然、明顯的
esthete（n.）唯美主義者、審美家
exceptionally（adv.）格外地、特別地
portrait（n.）人像、肖像

for example 例如
elderly people（n.）老人、年長者
education（n.）教育
sufficiently（adv.）充分地、足夠地

home, I would enjoy his latest photographs.

It was obvious to me that Wang was an esthete. All of his photographs were exceptionally beautiful, no matter whether a portrait or scenery, and gave me a kind of feeling that there was nothing not beautiful in his photographs. For example, in his portraits, it seemed that there were never elderly people with grey hair or missing teeth.

Wang Jiazheng had a special way for the education of his son. He wanted his son to be sufficiently imaginative, so he never gave him too many of the toys that were a mere copy of real-life objects. He often encouraged his son to pick an object at random and then imagine it to be something special. Sometimes I saw his son playing with a stick, but he insisted that it was a space-

---

imaginative（adj.）富想像力的、有創造力的
mere（adj.）僅僅的
real-life（adj.）真實的
encourage（v.）鼓勵

at random 隨便、任意
imagine（v.）想像
stick（n.）棍、棒
insist（v.）堅持、堅稱

空船就會長得這個樣子。

　　王小弟弟常常抱著他們家的小狗來找我，告訴我小狗今天心情不好，或者小狗今天和鄰居的狗吵架了。在我看來，小狗永遠是同樣的表情，這些都是王小弟弟一天到晚胡思亂想的結果。王嘉政卻不在意他兒子胡思亂想，他反而常和王小弟弟胡扯，他認為唯有如此，他的兒子才會有豐富的想像力。

　　王小弟弟是國小一年級的學生，每天走路上學，也走路回家，我們台中縣鄉下治安很好，絕大多數的國小

---

spaceship（n.）太空船、飛船　　expression（n.）表情、臉色
seek out 找、尋找　　　　　　　remark（n.）話語
mood（n.）心情、情緒　　　　　result（n.）結果、成果
perspective（n.）看法，觀點　　day-in, day-out 天天、日復一日

ship. He said that in the future spaceships would be just like this.

The Wang son, carrying the family dog, often sought me out. He would tell me that the little dog was not in a good mood today or that it had fought with the neighbor's dog. From my perspective, however, the dog's expression was always the same. The son's remarks were all the result of the day-in, day-out workings of his wild imagination. Wang however was not concerned about his son's imagination. In fact, he often talked nonsense with his son, thinking that in this way his son would have a fertile imagination.

Little Wang was in the first grade. He walked to and from school each day. Safety was no problem in Taichung County so the majority of elementary school

---

imagination（n.）想像力
concerned（adj.）擔心的、在意的
in fact 事實上、其實
nonsense（n.）胡説、胡扯
fertile（adj.）豐富的、豐饒的

grade（n.）年級
safety（n.）治安、安全
majority（n.）大多數
elementary school（n.）小學

學生都是如此上學的。王小弟弟每天這樣的來來回回，

他的談話內容就更加豐富了，每次我們吃飯的時候都會

聽到王小弟弟的見聞，但是也弄不清楚這些見聞是真是

假，因此我們都知道有些是出自他的想像。

　　王小弟弟常提到一位張爺爺，好像是一位慈祥的老

人家，很喜歡小孩子，會和小孩子玩。王小弟弟每次提

到張爺爺都很快樂，可是前些日子，王小弟弟提到張爺

爺的時候，他的表情變得比較嚴肅，因為他說：「張爺

爺生病了。」

　　有一天我們吃晚飯的時候，王小弟弟忽然問他的媽

媽，「媽媽，妳會祈禱嗎？」王太太說她會，於是王小

---

back and forth 來來回回　　　　　conversation（n.）談話、對話
enrich（v.）使豐富　　　　　　　report（n.）報告、描述

students went to school in this way. Every day Little Wang walked back and forth to school, and it enriched his conversation. Each time we had supper together we would always hear the son's report on what he had seen. But we were never sure if it was true or not for we all knew that some of it came from his imagination.

Little Wang often referred to a Grandpa Zhang, who seemed to be a kind old man who liked kids and played with them. Little Wang was very happy whenever he mentioned Grandpa Zhang, but recently, he became very serious when he referred to him because he said, "Grandpa Zhang is sick."

One day at supper, Little Wang suddenly asked his mother, "Mommy, are you able to pray?" Mrs. Wang

---

refer to 提到、談論
recently（adv.）最近、近來
serious（adj.）嚴肅的

suddenly（adv.）突然、忽然
pray（v.）禱告、祈禱

弟弟很嚴肅的請他媽媽替張爺爺祈禱，因為張爺爺的病情非常嚴重了。當天晚上，王小弟弟睡覺以後，我正和王嘉政在客廳裡聊天，突然聽到王太太的尖叫聲，原來王小弟弟不見了，我們發現王小弟弟穿了全套衣服鞋子從二樓房子跳了下去，他床上的棉被也不見了，顯然王小弟弟偷偷地穿好了衣服，順手拿了棉被溜了出去。

　　王太太當時嚇壞了，可是王嘉政卻不太慌，他叫我幫他忙，我們牽了小狗出去，小狗沿著王小弟弟上學的路，來到了一個小公園，公園裡什麼人也沒有，可是小狗一下子就將王小弟弟找到了。王小弟弟當時熟睡在一張石頭做成的桌子上，他旁邊睡了一位老人，雖然他也

---

illness（n.）疾病
extremely（adv.）非常、極端地
sharp（adj.）尖銳的
scream（n.）喊叫、尖叫
missing（adj.）失蹤的

discover（v.）發現、找到
blanket（n.）棉被、毯子
nowhere（adj.）不存在的、沒有的、哪裡都不
apparently（adv.）顯然

said that she was, so her son very seriously asked her to pray for Grandpa Zhang because his illness had become extremely serious. That evening after the son had gone to bed, I was talking with Jiazheng in the living room and suddenly heard Mrs. Wang's sharp scream. Little Wang was missing. We discovered that he had gotten out from the second floor fully clothed. His blanket was also nowhere to be seen. Apparently, the boy had secretly put on his clothes, taken his blanket, and snuck away.

Mrs. Wang was scared to death, but Jiazheng was not too alarmed and asked me to help. We took their little dog with us, and it followed Little Wang's usual way to school. We came to a small park that was deserted but the dog immediately found Little Wang. Little Wang was sound asleep on a stone table. Next to him was sleeping an old man. Even though he was also under a blanket, it was obvious that his clothes were old and

secretly（adv.）祕密地、背地裡
sneak away 溜走，悄悄離開
scared（adj.）害怕的、恐懼的
alarmed（adj.）受驚的、驚恐的

deserted（adj.）無人的、人煙罕至的
immediately（adv.）立刻、一下子
even though 雖然、儘管
obvious（adj.）明顯的、顯著的

蓋了被，但他的衣衫破舊卻非常的明顯，他的面容蒼老而憔悴，一望就知是王小弟弟所常提到的張爺爺，而張爺爺一定是個流浪漢。王嘉政請我將王小弟弟抱回去，在我走以前，他好像在設法推醒張爺爺，可是張爺爺似乎沒有被他推醒。

王小弟弟始終睡得很沉，我將他送回家，就離開了。王嘉政沒有回來，我知道他一直在照顧張爺爺。我當時在想，王小弟弟一定感到張爺爺病得非常之重，他要在這關鍵的一刻，和張爺爺睡在一起。我和王嘉政都以為張爺爺是王小弟弟的想像中的人物，沒有想到其實確有其人，而且是位老流浪漢。

---

worn（adj.）破舊的、磨損的　　figure out 設法、想出
vagrant（n.）流浪漢　　wake up 叫醒

worn. His face was old and tired. One look and we knew it was the Grandpa Zhang whom Little Wang talked about so often. And, Grandpa Zhang was indeed a vagrant. Jiazheng asked me to carry Little Wang back. Before I left, he was trying to figure out how to wake up Grandpa Zhang, but it seemed the old man couldn't be awakened.

Through it all Little Wang was sound asleep. I took him home and then left. When Jiazheng did not return, I knew that he was still looking after Grandpa Zhang. I was thinking that Little Wang definitely had felt that Grandpa Zhang's illness was extremely serious. It was at that moment that he wanted to sleep with Grandpa Zhang. Jiazheng and I had both thought that Grandpa Zhang was a character out of Little Wang's imagination. We did not think that there really was such a person, and one who was a vagrant.

---

awaken（v.）喚醒
look after 照顧、照料

definitely（adv.）肯定地、明確地
character（n.）人物

　　王嘉政說他叫了救護車將張爺爺送到醫院的急診

室，他從未醒過來，第二天早上在醫院裡過世了。王嘉

政從未離開張爺爺，他和附近的派出所聯絡，他們告訴

他，張爺爺有點頭腦不清楚，也從來沒有說過一句話，

所以他們無法知道他是誰、從哪裡來；他們幾次將他送

入遊民收容所，他卻常溜了出來在公園裡過夜，因為他

從不傷害人，警察就不管他了。過一陣子他會去派出所

一次，派出所的警察們會替他準備一些乾淨的衣服，附

近有些好心的人一直給他食物吃，他就在這個小鎮上生

活很多年了。

　　警察們說老流浪漢喜歡小孩子，奇怪得很，小孩子

---

ambulance（n.）救護車　　　　　police station（n.）警察局、派出所
emergency room（n.）急診室　　　a couple of times 好幾次
neighborhood（n.）鄰近、附近　　shelter（n.）收容所、避難所

Jiazheng said that he had called an ambulance to take Grandpa Zhang to the emergency room. He never woke up and died the next day in the hospital. Jiazheng never left Grandpa Zhang's side and contacted the neighborhood police station. The police told him that Grandpa Zhang was not all that clear in the head and had never spoken a word, so they never knew who he was or where he came from. A couple of times they had sent him to a shelter for the homeless, but he would always leave and spend the night in the park. The police never bothered him because he never hurt anyone. After a while, he would return to the police station and they would provide some clean clothes for him. Good-hearted people in the neighborhood always gave him something to eat. And so for many years he lived like this in this village.

The police said that the old vagrant liked little kids,

---

the homeless（n.）無家可歸的 人、遊民
provide（v.）提供、供給

good-hearted（adj.）好心的
village（n.）小鎮、村莊

也喜歡他，他們從來沒有交談，可是老先生好像會玩些

把戲，將那些調皮的頑童引得大樂。王小弟弟顯然就是

一個和老先生建立深厚友誼的小男孩。他說老先生姓

張，當然是出於他的想像。

王嘉政替張爺爺舉辦了正式的告別式，王小弟弟和

他的玩伴們由老師帶著，到張爺爺靈前恭恭敬敬地行

禮。對於我們大人，張爺爺是一位又老又窮的流浪漢，

可是對那些小孩子，張爺爺卻是一個愛他們的慈祥老

人。

王嘉政告訴我，張爺爺的這件事改變了他的很多想

法，他發現人類太注意表面的美麗，而忽略靈魂深處的

---

oddly（adv.）奇怪地　　　　　completely（adv.）完全地、徹底地
naughty（adj.）頑皮的、淘氣的　funeral（n.）喪禮、告別式
friendship（n.）友誼

and that, oddly enough, the kids liked him. They never talked, but the old man seemed to be able to play some games that left those naughty kids very happy. It was clear that Little Wang was one of the boys who developed a deep friendship with the old man. That he called him Mr. Zhang came completely from his imagination.

Jiazheng arranged for a funeral for Grandpa Zhang. Their teacher took Little Wang and his playmates to the funeral and they all very respectfully bowed before the coffin. For us adults, Grandpa Zhang was an old, poor vagrant, but for those children, he was a kind old man who loved them.

Jiazheng told me that the affair of Grandpa Zhang changed his thinking. He discovered that people pay too

---

playmate（n.）玩伴
respectfully（adv）恭敬地

bow（v.）鞠躬、行禮
coffin（n.）棺木、靈柩

善良，戴安娜王妃和德蕾莎修女幾乎同時去世，媒體卻獨鍾戴安娜王妃，就是最好的例子。對大人來說，張爺爺是個不值得注意的流浪漢，而對小孩來說，張爺爺是個慈祥的老人。王小弟弟的看法，使王嘉政常從別的角度來觀察事物。

以後，王嘉政的照片漸漸有了改變，在烈日下的勞動人民和老太婆，都成了他鏡頭追捕的目標。有一張黑白照片，特別傳神，照片中一個小孩和他的祖母玩一個遊戲，祖母滿臉皺紋，也沒有牙齒，衣服更是普通，可是她的慈祥和孩子對她的熱愛，全被收進了王嘉政的照片中。

---

exterior（adj.）外在的、外表的　　perspective（n.）看法、觀點
overlook（v.）忽略　　　　　　　angle（n.）角度
goodness（n.）善良、美德　　　　afterwards（adv.）以後，後來
media（n.）媒體　　　　　　　　gradually（adv.）漸漸地

much attention to exterior beauty and overlook the goodness deep in one's soul. Princess Diane and Mother Teresa both died about the same time. That the media only paid attention to Princess Diane is a very good example. For adults, Grandpa Zhang was a vagrant not worth any attention. But for children, he was a kind old man. It was the perspective of Little Wang that caused Jiazheng to look at things from a different angle.

Afterwards, the photographs of Jiazheng gradually began to change. Now the focus of his camera was to capture old women and other people laboring under the harsh sunlight. One black and white photo was particularly inspiring. It showed a child and his grandmother playing a game. The face of the grandmother had many wrinkles. She had no teeth and her clothes were simple, but her kindness and the love the child had for her were completely revealed by Jiazheng's photo.

---

focus（n.）焦點、目標
capture（v.）拍攝、捕捉
labor（v.）勞動
harsh（adj.）嚴酷的、惡劣的

inspiring（adj.）啟發靈感鼓舞人心
wrinkle（n.）皺紋
kindness（n.）慈祥、和藹
reveal（v.）顯示、披露

　　有一次王嘉政給我看他最近收藏的一座雕像，這座雕像是一位老婦人抱著一位死去的中年男子，老婦人是典型的鄉下婦人，滿臉哀慟的表情。他叫我猜這座雕像描寫的是誰，我猜不出來，也不知道它的來源。

　　原來這是米開朗基羅的傑作：《聖母抱耶穌》。我們所熟悉的聖母抱耶穌雕像，聖母極為年輕美麗，這是米開朗基羅年輕時的作品；可是他老了以後，了解耶穌去世的時候，聖母已是六十幾歲的老婦人，而且聖母出身貧寒，在鄉下一輩子，應該是位鄉下老婦人。所以他又雕刻了一座比較接近事實的聖母抱耶穌雕像。問題在於，世人不肯接受這座雕像，因為大家只喜歡看表面的美。這座雕像放在翡冷翠，可是遊客很少去看它。

---

statue（n.）雕像、雕塑
collect（v.）收集、收藏
typical（adj.）典型的、代表性的

peasant（n.）農夫、農民
mournful（adj.）悲傷的、哀慟的
masterpiece（n.）傑作、名作

Jiazheng showed me a statue he had recently collected. It was an old woman holding a dead, middle-aged man. The old woman was a typical peasant and her face had a mournful expression. He asked me to guess who this statue was of. I couldn't and did not know its origin.

It was Michelangelo's masterpiece of Mary holding her Son, the Pietà. The Pietà that we are familiar with shows a very young and beautiful Mary and is the work of the young Michelangelo. But in his old age, he realized that when Jesus left this world, his Mother was already an old woman in her sixties. Furthermore, Mary was born into poverty and spent her life in the countryside. She was an old peasant woman. Therefore he carved a statue that was closer to the real Mary holding Jesus. The problem is that people are not willing to accept this statue because everyone only likes exterior

familiar（adj.）熟悉的　　　　countryside（n.）鄉下、鄉間
furthermore（adv.）此外、而且　carve（v.）雕刻
poverty（n.）貧困、貧寒

　　我過去常常參觀大教堂，莊嚴的哥德式教堂和優美的現代化教堂，都是我的所愛，羅馬的聖彼得大教堂和伊斯坦堡的聖索菲亞大教堂，我都看過了。我一直心嚮往之的是西斯丁教堂，因為這是米開朗基羅有關《最後的審判》大壁畫的所在地。日前我終於如願以償，在西斯丁教堂瞻仰那些鬼斧神工的壁畫，這些壁畫，從藝術的眼光來看，的確是登峰造極之作，可是我發現我並未看了這些藝術品而大受感動。

　　我的心又飛到加爾各答的「垂死之家」，這是德蕾

---

tourist（n.）觀光客、遊客　　　　　Basilica（n.）大教堂
cathedral（n.）教堂　　　　　　　　fresco（n.）壁畫
solemn（adj.）莊嚴的、神聖的　　　the Last Judgment（n.）最後的審
Gothic（n.）哥德式建築　　　　　　判

beauty. The statue is in Firenze, but few tourists go to see it.

In the past I often visit cathedrals, both the solemn Gothic and the modern ones. I love both kinds. I've seen St. Peter's Basilica in Rome and the Santa Sophia in Istanbul. I've all along wanted to visit the Sistine Chapel, because this is where Michelangelo's frescos of the Last Judgment are. Recently I finally had chance to fulfill my wish and see the breathtaking frescos in the Sistine Chapel. These frescos, from an artistic perspective, are indeed magnificent works. But what I discovered was that it was not the artistic aspect that moved me so much.

My heart had turned to Calcutta's "Home for the

---

fulfill（v.）履行、實現
breathtaking（adj.）驚人的、鬼斧
神工的

artistic（adj.）藝術的
magnificent（adj.）宏偉的、登峰造
極的

莎修女為窮人所準備的地方，這裡看不到任何建築之美，可是在這裡，我可以感到人類最善良的一面。我永遠記得那些好心義工們握住垂死窮人手的畫面，這才是最美麗的畫面。而且這才使我想起最後審判，因為最後審判的時候，耶穌會問我：「當我需要你的時候，你有沒有握住我的手？」

當我步出西斯丁教堂的時候，我有一個很奇怪的想法，如果米開朗基羅復活了，而又重畫那幅巨型壁畫的時候，他也許會畫一幅簡單的畫，畫中只有德蕾莎修女握住一個乞丐的手。修女的滿面皺紋和乞丐的骨瘦如柴也許不美，可是他們一定能夠打動觀賞者的內心深處，而且能使人滿懷平安地離開西斯丁教堂。多可惜，世上

---

architectural（adj.）建築的   verge（n.）邊緣
volunteer（n.）義工、志願者   beggar（n.）乞丐

Dying," a place Mother Teresa had prepared for poor people. There is no architectural beauty there, but there I can feel the best goodness of people. I will forever remember the pictures of those good-hearted volunteers holding poor people on the verge of death. These are the most beautiful pictures.

And they make me think of the Last Judgment, because then Jesus will ask me, "Did you hold my hand when I needed you?"

As I was walking out of the Sistine Chapel, I had a strange thought. If Michelangelo were to be reborn and once again did those huge frescos, he probably would paint a simple picture of Mother Teresa holding the hand of a beggar. The wrinkles on Mother Teresa's face and the skinny beggar perhaps are not beautiful, but they can definitely move the inner depths of the heart of the observer and cause one to leave the Sistine Chapel filled

---

skinny（adj.）皮包骨的、極瘦的　　　observer（n.）觀賞者
inner（adj.）內心的、內在的

沒有一座有這幅壁畫的教堂。

　　感謝王小弟弟，我想我已經不像過去那樣地注意表面了。

——原載八十七年十二月十二日《聯合副刊》

---

shame（n.）可惜、遺憾　　　　no longer 不再

with peace. What a shame that on our earth there is not a church with such a fresco.

Thanks to Little Wang, I no longer as before only pay attention to the exterior of things.

---

pay attention to 注意

鎖

The Lock

鮑端磊　譯

　　老蔣拿出了鑰匙，打開了鎖，從裡面拿出了一個大大的罐子，罐子打開，裡面放的是白米，我們平時吃飯的米。

　　Old Jiang took out a key, undid the lock, and from inside removed a big jar. He opened that jar, and inside was the ordinary white rice that we eat all the time.

鎖

是用來鎖最珍貴的東西的。

　　我的好友老蔣有收藏的癖好，從小就如此，他的事業相當不錯，收藏的東西也就越來越值錢。每次到他家去，總會發現一些他的珍品，我對這些東西一竅不通，必須由他解釋。我記得他曾給我看把扇子，對我來講，這把扇子實在貌不驚人，後來才知道，扇子上的字是和珅這位大奸臣親筆寫的，當然有所值了。

lock（n.）鎖
secure（v.）保護、使安全
precious（adj.）珍貴的、寶貴的
possession（n.）財產、所有物
be fond of 喜歡、熱愛
extremely（adv.）十分、非常
collect（v.）收藏

beginning（n.）最初、一開始
business（n.）事業
successful（adj.）成功
increasingly（adv.）日益、逐漸
valuable（adj.）值錢的、貴重的
treasure（n.）寶物、珍品
crack（v.）破解、解開

Locks are used to secure our most precious possessions.

My good friend Old Jiang is extremely fond of collecting. He's been that way from the beginning. His business has been very successful and the things he has collected have become increasingly valuable. Every time I'm at his house I discover some new treasure. I can't crack the mystery of these things, though, just can't get the point. I need his words of explanation.

I recall he once showed me a fan, and as far as I could tell, the fan wasn't the least bit out of the ordinary. Afterwards I learned that the Chinese characters drawn on that fan came from the brush of the Qing dynasty corrupt official Heshen. Of course it was worth a mint.

mystery（n.）祕密
get the point 了解
explanation（n.）解釋、解說
recall（v.）回想、想起
fan（n.）扇子
as far as 到…的程度、就…而言
ordinary（n., adj.）普通、平凡
afterwards（n., adv.）後來、之後

character（n.）字、字體
draw（v.）寫、畫
brush（n.）毛筆、畫筆
dynasty（n.）朝代
corrupt（adj.）貪污的、腐敗的
official（n.）官員
mint（n.）一大筆錢

　　老蔣並不炫耀他的財富，他只是喜歡這些有價值的古董，他太太對這些東西也沒有什麼興趣，他的獨生兒子在輔仁大學社會系畢業，他知道這些古董的價值，可是並不想擁有這些東西。

　　老蔣的古董大多存放在保險箱裡，家裡客廳裡展示的只是一小部分，當然這個玻璃櫃是上鎖的，而且有一套保全系統，每次他要將任何一件古董拿出來給我們看，都必須先解除保全系統，然後用鑰匙打開鎖。

　　昨天我又去找老蔣聊天，聊了一陣，我問他，你家

flash（v.）炫耀
wealth（n.）財富
simply（adv.）只是
antique（n.）古董、古物
interest（n.）興趣
graduate（v.）畢業

sociology（n.）社會學
value（n.）價值
curio（n.）古董、珍品
desire（n.）欲望、渴望
possess（v.）擁有、占有
store（v.）存放、儲存

Old Jiang isn't one to flash his wealth around. He simply enjoys his antiques. His wife doesn't have any interest in these things. He has a son who graduated from the Sociology Department at Fu Jen University. He knows the value of these curios, but has no desire to possess them.

Most of Old Jiang's antiques are stored in safe deposit boxes, and the family living room displays only a small portion of his collection. The glass cabinet is of course locked. It is also protected by an alarm system. Every time he takes out some antique or the other to show us, he first must disconnect the alarm. Then he puts his key into the lock.

Yesterday I went to Old Jiang's for a chat and after we talked for a while, I asked him, "What's the most

safe deposit box（n.）保險箱　　cabinet（n.）櫥櫃
living room（n.）客廳　　　　　protect（v.）保護、防護
display（v.）展示、陳列　　　　alarm（n.）警報
portion（n.）部分　　　　　　　disconnect（v.）解除、切斷
collection（n.）收藏、收藏品　　chat（n.）聊天

裡最珍貴的東西是什麼？他眼睛一亮，帶我走進了他的

廚房，在廚房裡，有一大片的櫃子，每一扇櫃子的門都

不上鎖，唯獨有一扇門上了鎖。顯然裡面藏了一件珍貴

的東西，可是有什麼珍貴的東西會要放在廚房裡呢？

老蔣拿出了鑰匙，打開了鎖，從裡面拿出了一個大

大的罐子，罐子打開，裡面放的是白米，我們平時吃飯

的米。

為什麼這罐如此不值錢的米如此珍貴呢？原來老蔣

的兒子參加了台灣派駐到高棉的和平團，和平團的服務

對象全是最窮的人。有一次，他兒子送了一袋米給一位

---

twinkle（v.）閃亮

cupboard（n.）食櫥、碗櫃、櫥物櫃

apparently（adv.）顯然

undo（v.）打開、解開

remove（v.）拿開、搬開、搬移、移動

jar（n.）罐子

precious thing you've got here in the house?" His eyes twinkled as he led me into his kitchen. There in the kitchen were great cupboards with no locks on the doors. There was one door, however, that was locked. Apparently a very precious thing was stored inside, but what kind of valuable would be placed in a kitchen?

Old Jiang took out a key, undid the lock, and from inside removed a big jar. He opened that jar, and inside was the ordinary white rice that we eat all the time.

Why did this jar contain inexpensive rice as if it were a precious treasure?

Old Jiang's son was once active in a humanitarian service group that went to Cambodia. The humanitarian

---

contain（v.）包含、含有
inexpensive（adj.）便宜的、廉價的
active（adj.）活躍的、積極的

humanitarian（adj.）人道主義的、慈善的
Cambodia（n.）柬埔寨

可憐的寡婦，這位婦女的住處簡陋到了極點，沒有水，

沒有電，只有一張床放在泥地上。婦人拿到了米，高興

極了，將米藏到了床底下，老蔣兒子問她：「太太，妳

還需要什麼嗎？」婦人一直不願啟口，最後，她說了，

她要一把鎖，因為她家裡已經有值錢的東西了。

　　老蔣兒子的信改變了老蔣的想法，他要時時提醒他

自己，世界上有多少人連飯都沒有得吃，因此他將他的

米上了鎖，每天燒飯，必須開鎖才能拿出米來。他希望

他的子子孫孫都不會忽略一件事：對很多窮人而言，米

---

deliver（v.）傳送、運送　　　crude（adj.）粗陋的

widow（n.）寡婦　　　　　　poor（adj.）貧窮的、簡陋的

pitiful（adj.）可憐的　　　　hut（n.）小屋

group served the poorest of the poor. One day his son delivered a bag of rice to a widow in a pitiful situation. This woman was living in a crude, dirty poor hut that had neither water nor electricity. All she had was a bed sitting in the mud. The woman took the rice and, just as happily as could be, placed the bag under her bed. Old Jiang's son asked her, "Madame, what else do you need?"

For a while the woman wouldn't say a word. Then she said she wanted a lock for her door because her home finally had something worth money.

The letter old Jiang's son mailed him changed his way of thinking. From that time on, he resolved to always remember that the world had more than a few people who didn't even have the food they needed to survive. So he would keep his rice under lock and key. Every day he wanted to cook, well, he had to unfasten

---

electricity (n.) 電、電力
mud (n.) 泥、泥濘
resolve (v.) 決心、決定

survive (v.) 生存、存活
unfasten (v.) 解開

是最珍貴的東西。

　　我很欣賞老蔣的想法，看來他的兒子是不會看到那些曾經被老蔣上了鎖的珍品了，可是一定有更多的窮人家庭會要上鎖了。

——原載八十七年十一月《張老師月刊》

grandchildren（n.）孫子　　imaginable（adj.）能想像的
ignore（v.）忽視　　appreciate（v.）欣賞
fact（n.）事實

that lock just to get the rice out. He hoped his grandchildren would never ignore a fact: For many a poor person, rice was the most precious thing imaginable.

I really appreciate Old Jiang's idea. It seems his son wasn't able to see the treasures Old Jiang had locked up. Surely, however, there were many poor families that would also want a lock.

---

idea（n.）想法　　　　　　　　surely（adv.）一定、想必
lock up 鎖起來　　　　　　　　however（adv.）然而、可是

幕永不落下
The Curtain Never Goes Down

康士林　譯

你可以說我在演戲，可是演這一個角色，沒有台上台下，沒有前台後台；要演這個角色，幕就會永不落下。

Perhaps you could say that I'm acting. But in acting this part, there is no on-stage and off-stage, no audience and back-stage. For this part, the curtain never goes down.

我

到現在還記得我是如何認識張義雄的。

有一天，我開車經過新竹的光復路，忽然看到一位年紀非常大的老太太在路上滑倒了，而且顯然不能站起來，我停下車去扶她，正好有一個年輕人騎機車過來，他也停了下來幫我的忙。我們兩人一同將老太太抬進了我車子的後座，我請年輕人在後座照顧老太太，他立刻答應，這位年輕人就是張義雄。他陪我送老太太到省立新竹醫院去。

在路上，我從後視鏡看張義雄，我發現他有一種特

---

suddenly（adv.）突然、忽然　　come over 過來
fall down 跌倒、滑倒　　　　　lift（v.）舉起、抬起
moreover（adv.）此外、而且　　backseat（n.）後座
motorcycle（n.）摩托車、機車　look after 照料、照顧

I still remember how I had met Zhang Yixiong.

One day, as I was driving along Guangfu Road in Hsinzhu, I suddenly saw that a very old lady had fallen down on the road. Moreover, it was clear that she could not get up. I stopped my car and went to help her up. Just at this moment a young man was riding by on his motorcycle. He also stopped and came over to help me. The two of us lifted the old lady into the backseat of my car. I asked the young man to sit in the back and look after the elderly lady. He immediately agreed. This young man was Zhang Yixiong, and he accompanied me while I sent the elderly lady to the Hsinzhu Provincial Hospital.

On the way, I took a look at Zhang in the rearview

---

elderly（adj.）年老的、年長的
immediately（adv.）立刻、一下子
agree（v.）同意、答應
accompany（v.）陪同、伴隨

provincial（adj.）省的、省立的
rearview mirror（n.）後視鏡、照後鏡

別溫柔的表情，他輕輕地扶著老太太，讓老太太斜靠在他肩上，他也握住了老太太的手，雖然沒有講話，可是很顯然的，他在安慰她。

到了醫院，老太太被安置在一張床上，急診室的醫生說沒有任何問題，她只是老了。我於是設法打電話到附近的派出所去，告訴他們這位老太太的消息，巧得很，老太太的兒子正好到派出所去找人，他立刻趕到醫院來了。所謂兒子，也已七十歲了，可見老太太是九十歲左右的人。

就在我四處打電話的時候，張義雄寸步不離地看顧著老太太，並且緊緊地握住她的手，他的另一隻手一直

discover（v.）發現　　　　　　allow（v.）准許、允許
particularly（adv.）特別地　　shoulder（n.）肩膀
gentle（adj.）溫柔的、和順的　comfort（v.）安慰、慰問
manner（n.）態度、舉止　　　emergency room（n.）急診室

mirror and discovered that he had a particularly gentle manner. He gently held the elderly lady and allowed her to rest on his shoulder while he was also holding her hand. Although they did not speak, it was clear that he was comforting her.

After we arrived at the hospital, the woman was placed on a bed in the emergency room, where the doctor said that there was no problem. It's only that she is old. Next, I called the local police station and told them about this woman. Most coincidentally, the son of the woman had just gone to the station to look for her. He immediately came to the hospital. This "son" however was already seventy years old, so the woman was in her nineties.

As I was making phone calls to various places, Zhang Yixiong never left her and was taking care of her.

---

local（adj.）當地的
police station（n.）警察局、派出所
coincidentally（adv.）碰巧、巧合

look for 尋找
various（adj.）不同的、許多的
take care of 照顧、照料

在輕輕地拍拍老太太，老太太有時好像也在講一些話，我們誰也聽不懂她在說什麼。她的眼光幾乎沒有一分鐘離開過張義雄，張義雄的眼光也從不離開她。

老太太的兒子來了以後，我們就離開了。我送張義雄回到光復路去牽他的機車，在路上，我的好奇心來了，我問了他是不是一位神職人員。他如此有耐心，如此地溫柔，普通年輕男孩子是很少會這樣的。

張義雄聽了我的話，非常高興。他說，他不是神職人員，而是藝術學院戲劇系的學生，最有趣的是，他告訴我他在演戲，因為最近他要扮演一個神父的角色，所

---

tightly（adv.）緊緊地
pat（v.）輕拍
understand（v.）了解、明白

depart（v.）離開
curiosity（n.）好奇，好奇心
priest（n.）神父、神職人員

Moreover, with one hand, he was holding her hand tightly, while, with the other, he was gently patting her. At times, she seemed to be saying something. But none of us could understand what she was saying. Her eyes never left Zhang Yixiong for a single moment and his never left her.

After the elderly woman's son had come, I departed. I took Zhang Yixiong back to get his motorcycle on Guangfu Road. Out of curiosity, I asked him if he was a priest. He had a patience and gentleness that was rare for a young man of his age.

Hearing my question, he was very happy and said that he was not a priest, but was a student in the drama department of the College of Fine Arts. What was most interesting to me was that he told me that he was acting

---

patience（n.）耐心、耐性　　　interesting（adj.）有趣的
gentleness（n.）温柔、和善　　act（v.）演戲
drama department（n.）戲劇系

以他一上了車就開始扮演神父。他問我對他的演技印象

如何？我當然告訴他說，我一點兒也不知道他在表演。

　　張義雄又告訴我一件有趣的事，他說雖然他一開始

在表演，可是到了醫院以後，就不再演戲了，因為老太

太對他的依賴和信任，使他一分鐘也不敢離開她，何況

她又緊緊地握住了他的手。他覺得他在醫院裡的這一段

時光，是他的一種新的經驗，也會給他非常美好的回

憶。

　　張義雄是那種話很多的人，他告訴我他爸爸是清大

---

role（n.）角色　　　　　　　performance（n.）表演、演出
as soon as 一…，就…　　　naturally（adv.）當然、自然
perform（v.）表演、扮演　　respond（v.）回答、回應
impression（n.）印象　　　　beginning（n.）開始、最初

and soon he was to play the role of a priest. So, as soon as he got into the car, he started to perform the role of a priest. He asked what impression I had of his performance. I naturally responded that I did not know at all that he was performing.

He then told me one more interesting thing. Even though he was performing a role at the beginning, once he arrived at the hospital, it was no longer a role. The elderly woman's dependence on, and trust in, him caused him not to want to leave her for a single moment. Moreover, she was holding his hand very tightly. He felt that the time in the hospital was a kind of new experience for him, and it gave him a very beautiful memory.

Zhang Yixiong was a very talkative person. He told me that his father was a professor in the Information

---

no longer 不再
dependence on 信賴、依賴
trust in 相信、信任
experience（n.）經驗

memory（n.）回憶、記憶
talkative（adj.）健談的、多話的
professor（n.）教授
Information Science（n.）資訊科學

資訊系的教授，原來我和他爸爸是朋友，天下就有這麼

巧的事。

　　以後，我好幾次去看張義雄的表演，我是外行人，

沒有資格說他是不是非常好的演員，只是覺得他演什麼

像什麼。他爸爸告訴我張義雄很認真，演神父以前真的

找了一位神父和他住二個星期，也研究了教義。又有一

次，他要演一個築路工人，這次他真的去做了一個星期

的苦工，難怪他演得不錯了。

　　　令我吃驚的是，張義雄居然要去做神父了。如此活

---

turn out 原來、結果　　　　accurately（adv.）準確地、精確地
coincidence（n.）巧合　　　dedicated（adj.）認真的、專注的
outside of（n.）在…之外　　as well as 也，同樣
competence（n.）能力

Science Department of Tsinghua University. As it turned out, his father and I were friends. Such are the coincidences in our world.

Afterwards, I went a number of times to see Zhang Yixiong perform. Acting is outside of my competence, so I had no right to say whether or not he was a good actor. I could only say that he performed his role accurately. His father told me that his son was very dedicated. Before he performed his role as a priest, he had found a priest and lived with him for two weeks as well as also studied Christian doctrine. Then there was the time when he was to play a worker on road construction. That time he really went and spent a week doing hard labor. No wonder his acting was so successful.

What left me very surprised was that Zhang Yixiong finally did decide to become a priest. I was

---

Christian doctrine（n.）基督教教義　　no wonder 難怪
construction（n.）建造、建築　　successful（adj.）成功
labor（n.）勞動、勞工　　surprised（adj.）驚訝、訝異

潑好動的男孩子，肯去做神父，我當然感到很好奇，後來和他爸爸聯絡的結果，知道張義雄由於演戲的原因而認識了一些神父，也因此就變成了天主教徒。對於他決定去做神父，也不太意外，因為他知道張義雄雖然看上去嘻嘻哈哈，其實是一個很認真、很嚴肅的人。

很多年以後，我應邀去參加張義雄的祝聖神父大典，典禮莊嚴隆重，有一段時光，張義雄要完全伏在地上，看上去極為戲劇化。我當時心中在想：「張義雄，張義雄，你不要又在演戲了。」

我知道張義雄一開始的工作是替大專同學服務，他

curious（adj.）好奇
lively（adj.）活潑、生氣勃勃
active（adj.）積極、主動
preparation（n.）準備
as for 至於

decision（n.）決定
unexpected（adj.）想不到、出乎意外的
indeed（adv.）的確、其實

quite curious how it was that a young man so lively and active was willing to become a priest. Later, after contacting his father, I learned that his son had become a Catholic because of his meeting some priests in preparation for his role. As for his decision to become a priest, it was not unexpected because his father knew that his son was indeed a very dedicated and serious person, even though there were many smiles and much laughter on the outside.

Many years later, I accepted an invitation to go to Zhang Yixiong's ordination as a priest. The ceremony was very solemn and dignified, and at one point he had to prostrate himself on the ground, which was most dramatic. At that time I was thinking, "Zhang Yixiong, Zhang Yixiong, please don't be acting again."

I learned that Zhang Yixiong's first work as a priest

---

laughter（n.）大笑、笑聲
invitation（n.）邀請
ordination（n.）聖職的任命
ceremony（n.）典禮、儀式

solemn（adj.）莊嚴
dignified（adj.）隆重
prostrate（v.）俯臥、拜倒
dramatic（adj.）戲劇化

會唱歌，會彈吉他，大專學生當然很容易地就認同了
他。一年以後，他忽然說，他希望將主耶穌的光和熱，
帶到世界最黑暗的角落去，因此他已得到了主教的首
肯，要去監獄傳教了。他也曾寫信給我，說他要努力地
扮演一個好神父的角色。他知道這個工作是很困難的。

　　我常和張義雄的爸爸聯絡，他說張義雄雖然非常認
真，非常努力，卻不能為很多受刑人所接受，他們對他
的反應可以用「冷淡」兩個字來形容。可是前個星期，
我在報上看到一則消息，說張義雄神父如何地受到監獄
裡受刑人的歡迎，好多人就是喜歡參加他做的彌撒。

---

guitar（n.）吉他　　　　　　　bishop（n.）主教
relate（v.）認同、溝通、交流　permission（n.）同意、允許
warmth（n.）溫暖　　　　　　difficult（adj.）困難
accordingly（adv.）因此、於是

was to look after college students. He could sing and play the guitar so it would of course be easy for college students to relate to him. A year later, he suddenly said that he hoped to take the light and warmth of our Lord Jesus to the darkest corners of our world. Accordingly, he received his bishop's permission to do work in a prison. He also wrote to me and said that he wanted to play the role of a good priest. He knew that this work was very difficult.

I often contacted Zhang Yixiong's father who said that even though his son was very dedicated and devoted to his prison work, many prisoners did not respond well to his efforts. One word can describe the prisoners' response: "Indifference." Last week, however, I read a newspaper article that described how Father Zhang was very well received by the prisoners. Many of them liked to go to his Mass.

---

devoted（adj.）虔誠、致力　　response（n.）回應、反應
effort（n.）努力　　　　　　indifference（n.）冷淡、冷漠
describe（v.）形容、描述　　Mass（n.）彌撒

　　我打通了關節，讓那所監獄的典獄長請我去參觀，我的最重要目的，是要看看那位張神父，究竟是為什麼能受到如此的歡迎。參觀到一半，我看到一位工友模樣的人在洗廁所，他抬起頭來，忽然叫了起來，「你不就是李教授嗎？」我也立刻認出他來，原來我們的張神父在洗廁所，我當時幾乎講不出話來。

　　典獄長告訴我，張神父的確變成了監獄裡的工友，我發現他什麼事都做，洗廁所，掃地，擦玻璃窗，修剪花木。他住在監獄裡，和受刑人一起吃飯，當然他是一位神父，每天都做彌撒，而且監獄裡安排了時間，使他下午都在替一些念書的受刑人補習功課，他也在晚上講

---

connections（n.）關係、人脈
warden（n.）典獄長、管理員
main（adj.）主要的
purpose（n.）目的

exactly（adv.）正好、確切
half-way 一半、半途
janitor（n.）工友

Using all of my connections, I had the prison warden invite me to visit. My main purpose was to see exactly how it was that Fr. Zhang was so well received by the prisoners. Half-way through my tour I saw what seemed to be a janitor cleaning a toilet. He looked up and called out, "Aren't you Professor Lee?" I immediately recognized him. So it was that our Fr. Zhang was cleaning the toilets. I was almost speechless.

The warden told me that Fr. Zhang had indeed become the prison's janitor. I discovered that he was doing all kinds of things: cleaning toilets, sweeping floors, washing windows, trimming bushes. He lived in the prison and ate with the prisoners. Since he was a priest, he had Mass every day. The prison arranged the time so that he could have class for the prisoners who were studying in the afternoon and then have Mass and

---

toilet（n.）廁所、洗手間　　　　sweep（v.）打掃
recognize（v.）認出　　　　　　trim（v.）修剪、整理
speechless（adj.）無言、説不出話　bush（n.）灌木

道。雖然他是神父，他也是不折不扣的工友。

　　當我離開的時候，張義雄送我，和我殷殷道別，我問他為什麼這次成功了？他說，他這一次扮演的是耶穌基督本人，他想了很久，終於想通了，如果耶穌基督來到這個世界，他不會高高在上地講道，他一定會謙卑地替大家服務。因此他決定做一個工友，從洗廁所做起，而且他全天候地住在監獄裡。很多受刑人都離開了監獄，只有張神父幾乎永不離開。連除夕夜，也留了下來。年初二，他回家去和家人團圓，可是立刻又回來了。

　　我問他：「你是不是又在演戲了？」

---

preach（v.）講道、佈道　　　　　Jesus Christ（n.）耶穌基督
warmly（adv.）溫暖地、親切地　　eventually（adv.）最後、終於

preach in the evening. Although he was a priest, he was also a real janitor.

As I was leaving, Father Zhang saw me off and warmly said good-bye. I asked him why he was successful this time. He said that this time he was acting the part of Jesus Christ. He had thought about it for a long time and eventually saw the light. If Jesus Christ came to our world, he would not be preaching from on high. He would indeed be humbly serving everyone. Therefore he decided to become a janitor. He began by cleaning toilets and living all day in the prison. Many prisoners left the prison. It was only Fr. Zhang who never did. Even on the eve of the Lunar New Year, he was still there. On the second day of the New Year, he returned home to be with his family, but immediately returned to his prison.

I asked him, "Are you still acting?"

---

humbly（adv.）謙卑地
serve（v.）服務、服侍

eve（n.）前一天晚上、前夕
Lunar New Year（n.）農曆新年

張義雄說：「你可以說我在演戲，可是演這一個角色，沒有台上台下，沒有前台後台；要演這個角色，幕就會永不落下。」

要離開監獄，必須要走過好幾道門，有一道鐵門，是受刑人絕不能越過的，張義雄就在這道門前停了下來。我走了出去，他留了下來，他在裡面向外面的我揮手道別，我終於了解「幕永不落下」是什麼意思。

——原載八十七年七月十七日《聯合副刊》

---

perhaps（adv.）也許、或許
on-stage and off-stage 台上台下
audience（n.）觀眾

back-stage（n.）後台
curtain（n.）布幕、簾幕
steel（n.）鐵

He said, "Perhaps you could say that I'm acting. But in acting this part, there is no on-stage and off-stage, no audience and back-stage. For this part, the curtain never goes down."

In leaving the prison you have to go through many doors. There is one steel door that the prisoners are forbidden to go through. Zhang Yixiong stopped in front of this door. I walked through and he remained behind. He waved to me from inside as I went to the outside. Now I know the meaning of "the curtain never goes down."

---

forbidden（adj.）被禁止
in front of 在…之前
remain（v.）留下、待下

inside（n.）裡面、內部
outside（n.）外面、外部
meaning（n.）意思、意義

棉　襖
A Padded Chinese Jacket

鮑端磊　譯

　　張伯伯給我看一件好舊好舊的棉襖，他顯然早已不穿這件舊衣服了，但是看起來這件棉襖卻十分有特別的意義。

　　Uncle Zhang had me take a look at an indescribably old Chinese jacket with thick cotton padding, what we call a *mian au*. It was obvious he hadn't worn that jacket for ages. Clearly, however, that *mian au* meant something very special to him.

我 們學校裡有一位老工友，退伍軍人，我們稱他為張伯伯。春節以前，我要到大陸的杭州去參加一個學術會議，張伯伯聽說以後，來找我，說有事要請我幫忙。

張伯伯給我看一件好舊好舊的棉襖，他顯然早已不穿這件舊衣服了，但是看起來這件棉襖卻十分有特別的意義。

原來張伯伯曾經參與過徐蚌會戰，當時戰況非常慘烈，張伯伯的部隊曾經有一段時間被共軍團團圍住，雖然我們的空軍也試圖空投糧食和彈藥，但是常常空投到

retired（adj.）已退休的、已退職的、已退役的
soldier（n.）士兵、軍人
festival（n.）節日、喜慶日
scholarly（adj.）學者的、學者風度的、學術的

assistance（n.）援助、幫助
certain（adj.）某種（或一定）幫忙的
favor（n.）善意的行為、恩惠
indescribably（adv.）難以形容地、無法描述地
jacket（n.）夾克、上衣

Our school has a worker getting up in years now, a retired soldier we call Uncle Zhang. Before the Chinese New Year Festival, when he heard I was to go to Hangzhou in mainland China for a scholarly meeting, Grandpa Zhang came to see me. Could I be of assistance to him by doing a certain favor?

Uncle Zhang had me take a look at an indescribably old Chinese jacket with thick cotton padding, what we call a *mian au.* It was obvious he hadn't worn that jacket for ages. Clearly, however, that *mian au* meant something very special to him.

When he was a soldier many years ago, Uncle Zhang took part in the battle of Xubang, the turning point of the Chinese civil war, the battle that marked the end of nationalist dominance in northern China (1948-

---

thick（adj.）茂密的、密集的
padding（n.）墊塞、填料
obvious（adj.）明顯的、顯著的
clearly（adv.）顯然地、無疑地
battle（n.）戰鬥、戰役
civil（adj.）國內的

nationalist（adj.）民族獨立主義的、民族主義(者)的、國家主義(者)的
dominance（n.）優勢、支配（地位）、統治（地位）
northern（adj.）北方的、向北方的、來自北方的

了敵人的陣地，所以張伯伯經常活在飢寒交迫，既無糧

草，又缺彈藥的情況之中。有一天，一批共軍對他們突

擊，張伯伯他們將對方擊退了，雖然暫時可以喘口氣，

但是張伯伯不僅感到又冷又餓，最嚴重的是他感到非常

的口渴，而他僅存的一些飲水也快喝到最後一滴了。

張伯伯看到一位剛才被他打死的共軍士兵，他腰上

有一個水壺，張伯伯就跑去拿這一個水壺。在張伯伯設

法解下水壺的時候，他發現這個小兵還帶了不少的乾

糧。當時天氣越來越冷，而小兵穿了一件很好的棉襖。

---

fighting（n.）戰鬥、戰爭

fierce（adj.）猛烈的、激烈的

battalion（n.）軍隊

surround（v.）包圍、圍困

Communist（adj.）共產黨的

guerilla（n.）游擊隊(員)

supply（n.）供給、供應

enemy（adj.）敵人的、敵方的

line（n.）界線、戰線

material（n.）物質、物品

hostile（adj.）敵人的、敵方的

territory（n.）領土、版圖

spell（n.）一段持續時間

fate（n.）命運、遭遇

freeze（v.）受凍

starve（v.）挨餓、飢餓

49). The fighting was fierce. For a period of time, Uncle Zhang's battalion found itself actually surrounded by Communist guerillas. Although our air force tried to drop food and medical supplies and such behind the enemy lines, often the material landed in hostile territory. So, for quite a spell Uncle was caught between the fate of freezing to death or starving. His condition was truly desperate. There were no necessities of life, and they lacked ammunition.

At one point in that predicament, a group of Communist infantrymen attacked his battalion, but Uncle Zhang and his comrades were able to drive the enemy back. Although the men could take a brief break, Uncle Zhang wasn't only cold and hungry. He was practically

---

condition（n.）情況、(健康等)狀態
desperate（adj.）危急的、絕望
的、險惡的
necessities（n.）必需品
lack（v.）缺少、不足、沒有
ammunition（n.）彈藥、軍火
predicament（n.）困境、危境
infantryman（n.）步兵

battalion（n.）營、大隊、協同作戰
的部隊、軍隊
comrade（n.）夥伴、同事
enemy（n.）敵人、仇敵、敵軍
brief（adj.）短暫的
break（n.）中斷、中止、休息
practically（adv.）幾乎、差不多、
事實上

張伯伯認為小兵已經死了，他就剝下這件棉襖，穿在軍

服裡面，他甚至還將這位小兵的鞋子也據為己有了。

張伯伯說，如果不是這件棉襖以及那個小兵的水壺

和乾糧，張伯伯可能會凍死，也可能因為缺水缺糧而死

die（v.）死亡　　　　　　　　waist（n.）腰、腰部
thirst（n.）渴、口渴　　　　　grab（v.）攫取、抓取
canteen（n.）（士兵等用的）水壺　　unfasten（v.）解開、鬆開
spot（v.）認出、發現　　　　　loop（n.）圈、環

dying of thirst. He had emptied his canteen down to the very last drop.

Uncle Zhang spotted a Communist soldier he had just shot to death. He had a canteen tied to his waist. Grandpa ran over to the body and grabbed that canteen. As he unfastened the loops of the canteen, he discovered the soldier was still carrying some dry rations. The weather those days was getting increasingly frigid, and so the soldier had been wearing a fine jacket, a mian au. In Uncle Zhang's mind, the fellow was already gone. He stripped off the *mian au* and put it on beneath his outer layer of clothes. He even took the shoes the soldier had on his feet.

Uncle Zhang told me that if he hadn't gotten the soldier's mian au and canteen, oh, and those dry rations,

---

discover（v.）發現、找到
rations（n.）口糧
increasingly（adv.）漸增地、越來越多地

frigid（adj.）寒冷的、嚴寒的
fellow（n.）男人、傢伙、人
strip（v.）剝、剝去、剝光
beneath（prep.）在……之下

在戰場上。所以他一直帶著這件棉襖，因為他一直對棉

襖的主人心存感激。

　　張伯伯突圍以後，在棉襖裡發現了棉襖主人的名字

和家鄉。這位小兵的家人將他的名字和住址寫在一張小

紙片上，而這張小紙片就塞在棉襖裡層的一個口袋裡。

小兵的名字叫做李少白，他的家鄉是浙江省白際山裡的

一個小村落。

　　雖然張伯伯對李少白心存感激，卻不敢和他的家人

聯絡，因為是他開槍將李少白打死的，當時他自己只有

---

probably（adv.）大概、或許、很
可能
frozen（adj.）冰凍的、極冷的、凍
僵的
battlefield（n.）戰場、戰地

original（adj.）最初的、本來的
jam（n.）困境、窘境
hometown（n.）故鄉、家鄉
stuff（v.）裝、填、塞

he'd have probably frozen to death. Without food or water, he'd have died on the battlefield. So since then, wherever he went, he always took that *mian au* along with him. Deep in his heart he always felt thankful for the original owner of that jacket.

Some time after Uncle Zhang had gotten out of that jam, he found the name of the soldier who owned that *mian au* inside the jacket, and the name of his hometown too. The soldier's family had written his name and address on a small card and stuffed the card deep between the lining of an inside pocket. The soldier's name was Li Shaobai. His hometown was an obscure village in Baiji Mountain in Zhejiang province.

Although Uncle Zhang was very grateful to Li Shaobai, he dared not establish contact with his family.

---

lining（n.）襯裡、內襯、內層
pocket（n.）口袋
obscure（adj.）隱匿的、偏僻的
village（n.）村莊、村
province（n.）省

grateful（adj.）感謝的、感激的
dare（v.）敢、膽敢
establish（v.）建立、取得
contact（n.）交往、聯繫、聯絡

十九歲，他的感覺是李少白死的時候也只有十幾歲。張伯伯來台灣雖然一開始也很苦，可是現在孫子已經在念清大的電機系，他雖然過得很好，卻一直記掛著李少白的家人，不知道他們生活得怎麼樣。

他給了我一筆錢，叫我帶到大陸去交給李少白的家人，他說大陸鄉下人多半住在老地方，我應該找得到這個地方的。張伯伯請我務必告訴李少白的家人，他雖然打死了李少白，他卻絕對和李少白無冤無仇，他家很

reckon（v.）覺得、猜想
fair（adj.）相當多的
suffering（n.）勞苦、苦難的經歷、令人痛苦的事

major（v.）主修
electrical（adj.）與電有關的、電氣科學的

The reason is that it was his gun that took that man's life. At the time he himself was only 19 years old. He reckoned that Li Shaobai was probably in his late teens when his life ended.

Now, he might have faced a fair amount of suffering in the beginning when he first came to Taiwan, but Uncle Zhang already had a grandson now majoring in Electrical Engineering at Tsinghua University. Although things had panned out well for him, thoughts of Li Shaobai's family had always gnawed at his heart. He hadn't a clue as to how their lives had turned out.

He gave me a certain amount of money, telling me to take it to the mainland and give it to Li Shaobai's loved ones. He said that out in the countryside, people generally lived for years and years in the same place. I ought to be able to find their place alright, he thought.

---

engineering（n.）工程、工程學
gnaw（v.）使煩惱、折磨
clue（n.）線索、跡象、提示

countryside（n.）鄉間、農村
generally（adv.）通常、一般地
alright（adv.）沒問題地

窮，當兵是迫不得已的事，當時他也弄不清他為什麼要

打共產黨，他也相信李少白和他一樣，一心一意只想早

日打完仗，好回去耕田。他說：「我們都是小老百姓，

我們小老百姓之間是沒有仇恨的，是大人物叫我們打仗

的，我們又有什麼辦法呢？」

我在杭州開完會以後，就去白際山了。我們開會的

時候，我逢人就問白際山怎麼去，沒有一位知道。我只

有自己想辦法，換了好幾種交通工具，最後包了一部汽

---

stretch（n.）延伸、擴大　　　poverty（n.）貧窮、貧困
imagination（n.）空想、妄想、幻想　stricken（adj.）受害的、受挫折的
consider（v.）考慮、細想　　　position（n.）形勢、境況、處境

Uncle Zhang asked me to tell Li's family that he may have killed Shaobai, but by no stretch of the imagination did he consider him his enemy. He himself came from a poverty-stricken family. Joining the army was simply impossible to avoid. In those days he had no clear idea of just why he was fighting the Communists. He also believed Li Shaobai was in the same position. He too was determined to end the war thing as quickly as possible, return home, and work as a farmer. He put it this way: "We were just ordinary people, and between ordinary people there is no feeling of enmity. It was the big wheels who pushed us into that war. What could we do?"

After my meeting ended in Hangzhou, I headed for Baiji Mountain. While I was still at the meeting I asked people how I could get to Baiji Mountain. No one knew. In the end, I just figured it out on my own. I hopped back and forth from one form of transport to the other

---

determine（v.）使決定、使下決心
ordinary（adj.）普通的、平凡的
hop（v.）跳上、快速移動

forth（adv.）向前、向前方
transport（n.）交通工具

車往白際山上的那個小村落駛去。

　　李少白的老家在山上，說實話，這裡不僅落後，而且也相當的荒涼，上山的公路顛得厲害，一路上看不到幾戶人家，汽車更是幾乎完全看不到，偶然可以看到公共汽車帶人上下山。因為是冬天，所有的樹木都沒有葉子，這部汽車似乎沒有什麼暖氣，虧得我穿了一件羽毛衣，再加上當天有太陽，我還不覺得太冷。村莊到了，我們東問西問，居然找到了李少白的家。鄉下人很少看到汽車來訪，紛紛出來看我這個不速之客是何許人也。

---

hire（v.）雇、雇用
outskirts（n.）郊外、郊區
simply（adv.）只是

downright（adv.）完全地、徹底地
desolate（adj.）荒蕪的、無人煙的
single（adj.）獨特的、唯一的

and finally found myself in a hired car on the road to that little village on the outskirts of Baiji Mountain.

Li Shaobai's old home was on the side of a mountain. To tell you the truth, it was not simply a place in the middle of nowhere. It was downright desolate out there. The road leading into the mountain was a single stretch of twists and turns, and from the road itself you couldn't even see places for people to live. In fact, you could hardly see any vehicles on the road.

Eventually I caught sight of a public bus taking people up and down the mountain. It was winter time, so all the trees were bare of leaves. It turned out the car didn't have a heater. Luckily for me, I was wearing a thick down sweater. And, after all, it was a sunny day, so I really didn't feel very cold.

We arrived at the village and after asking everyone

---

stretch（n.）延亙、連綿
twist（n.）轉彎、彎曲、曲折
vehicle（n.）車輛

bare（adj.）光禿禿的
sweater（n.）毛線衣

　　這個家似乎人很多，其中有一位長者，他行動不便，必須靠拐杖才能走路，他招呼我坐下。我忽然緊張了起來，不知該如何啟口。我結結巴巴地將張伯伯的故事講完，也完整地轉述了張伯伯那段「小老百姓彼此無冤無仇」的談話，最後我拿出了那張已經發黃的紙片，上面有「李少白」三個字。

　　老先生將那張紙片拿去看，整個屋子的人鴉雀無

folk（n.）人民、鄉民、同胞
strange（adj.）陌生的、生疏的、不熟悉的
gentleman（n.）先生、男士

cane（n.）手杖、枴杖
anxiety（n.）焦慮、掛念
flood（v.）湧上、湧現、湧出

in sight, sure enough, we found the family of Li Shaobai. People out there in the countryside rarely see a car arrive with a visitor. One by one, folks came out to take a look at just what this strange visitor looked like.

Actually, this family was very large. There was an elderly gentleman who couldn't get around very well. He needed a cane for walking. He asked me to take a seat. Suddenly a wave of anxiety flooded over me. I didn't know how to open my mouth. I stuttered and stammered and finally manageed to get Uncle Zhang's story out. I hammered home the point Uncle had made about the two men being just common, ordinary people without the slightest amount of animosity between them. Then, finally, I pulled out the old card, now all yellow. On it were written the characters, "Li Shaobai."

The elderly gentleman picked that card up in his

---

stutter（v.）結結巴巴地說話
stammer（v.）口吃、結結巴巴地說話
manage（v.）設法做到、勉力完成

hammer（v.）反覆強調
animosity（n.）仇恨、敵意、憎惡
character（n.）國字、字體

聲，都在等他說話。老先生的手有一點兒抖，他看了這張紙片以後，終於說話了，他說：「我就是李少白，我沒有死。」

故事是這樣的，李少白在前一天的戰鬥中被一槍打中了大腿，當場就完全不能動了，一步也不能走，連爬都不能。他的連長找了兩個其他的小兵，將他放上了一個擔架，蓋上一床棉被，叫這兩個小兵將他送到後方的一個醫護站去。

李少白有一個伙伴，在李少白快離開的時候，這個

---

silent（adj.）寂靜無聲的
tremble（v.）發抖、震顫
slightly（adv.）輕微地、稍微地、微小地
scrutinize（v.）細看，細閱
battle（n.）戰鬥、戰役

shot（n.）彈丸、砲彈
thigh（n.）股、大腿
crawl（v.）爬、爬行
company（n.）連
commander（n.）指揮官、司令官
buck（adj.）（某一軍銜等級中）最

hand and looked at it. The whole room had fallen as silent as could be. They were waiting for him to speak. The elderly man's hands trembled slightly. After he had scrutinized that card, he finally had something to say, and what he said was, "I am Li Hsaobai. I didn't die."

The story goes like this. The day before the battle, Li Shaobai caught a shot in the middle of his thigh and couldn't move. He couldn't even crawl on the ground, let alone take a step. His company commander called over a couple of buck privates, and had them lay him flat on a stretcher. They covered him with a blanket. The commander ordered the men to take Li Shaobai back to the medical station.

As Li Shaobai was about to leave the scene, a buddy of his asked him for his canteen and dry rations.

低一級的
private（n.）士兵
flat（adj.）平伏的、平臥的
stretcher（n.）擔架
cover（v.）遮蓋、覆蓋
blanket（n.）毛毯、毯子

order（v.）命令、叫
medical（adj.）醫療的
scene（n.）（事件發生的）地點、現場
buddy（n.）好朋友、夥伴、搭擋

軍中伙伴請他給他水壺和乾糧，因為後方不會缺水缺糧的，李少白不僅給了他水和乾糧，也給了他棉襪和鞋子，他反正短時間已經不可能走路，而且棉被也夠暖。他完全沒有想到他的伙伴第二天就陣亡了。他雖然到了醫護站，卻成了殘障者，走路要靠拐杖，解放軍給了他一筆錢，叫他回家。他有時也曾想到他的那位伙伴，但不知如何和他聯絡，今天才知道伙伴早已離開了人世。

老人的一番話，使我不知該說什麼，我決定不提張

figure（v.）認為、以為、估計　　　　shoe（n.）鞋
shortage（n.）缺少、不足、匱乏　　disabled（adj.）殘廢的、有缺陷的
jacket（n.）夾克、上衣　　　　　　cane（n.）手杖、枴杖

He figured that back of the line of fire there would be no shortage of water or food. Li gave him not only his water and rations but also his jacket and shoes. After all, it looked like he wouldn't be back on his feet walking around for a while. And the blanket over him was warm enough already. It never occurred to him that his friend would get killed the next day.

Although he made it to the medical station, as things turned out, he wound up disabled. For the rest of his life, he would need a cane to get around. The Liberation Army gave him a bit of money and sent him home. As time went on, he thought of his friend now and again, but had no idea how to get in touch with him. It was only today that he had learned that his old buddy left our world so early.

The elderly gentleman's words left me speechless. I decided not to mention the money that Uncle Zhang had

---

liberation（n.）解放
army（n.）軍隊

speechless（adj.）一時說不出話來的
mention（v.）提到、說起

伯伯託我帶錢來的事，因為我擔心老人家會怕觸楣頭，

還好李老先生打破了僵硬的氣氛，叫人弄來一大碗熱騰

騰的粥，也弄來了一些小菜，招呼我們吃。我吃得津津

有味，從來沒有想到可以用粥來招待訪客。

李老先生問我張伯伯在台灣生活的情形，我告訴他

張伯伯在軍中時當然很苦，退伍以後，生活稍微改善了

一些，最近是很舒服的了，不愁吃，不愁穿。

李老先生說他苦了一輩子，因為他是個農人，卻不

---

rigid（adj.）嚴格的、死板的、苛刻的
atmosphere（n.）氣氛
steaming（v.）冒熱氣、熱騰騰的、蒸氣騰騰的

congee（n.）稀飯、粥
side（adj.）次要的、附帶的、從屬的
dishes（n.）菜餚

sent along with me. I was worried the old fellow would fear it might bring him bad luck.

Happily enough, the elderly Mr. Li broke the rigid atmosphere in the room. He had someone bring me a big steaming bowl of congee. Then came some side dishes. "Go ahead now and eat," he said. I ate with relish. I had never imagined you could use congee to welcome a guest.

Old Mr. Li asked me how Uncle Zhang's life had panned out in Taiwan. I told him that his time as a soldier was of course tough for him. After he got out of the army, his life improved a little. In recent years he had it pretty good, though. He had what he needed, food, clothes, and so on.

Old Mr. Li said his whole life had been a hard go.

---

relish（n.）津津有味、風味、滋味
imagine（v.）猜想、料想
pan out（ph.）成功
tough（adj.）艱難的

improve（v.）改善、變好
recent（adj.）最近的、近來的
though（adv.）然而、還是、不過

能種田，虧得他太太始終對他非常好，他的家人也一直沒有嫌棄他。

我告訴李老先生張伯伯的兩個兒子都是工人，但孫子都受了良好的教育，其中有一位還是新竹清華大學電機系的學生。

李老先生一聽到這些，忽然興奮了起來，他說他的兒子們都是農人，但有一個孫子快上大學了。這個孫子極為聰明，縣政府給他獎學金，使他能到城裡的高中去念書，他今年高三，模擬考的分數非常高，一定可以進

farmer（n.）農夫
wound（n.）創傷、傷、傷口、傷疤
fortunately（adv.）幸運地、僥倖地
bear（v.）懷有、心懷（某種情緒意念）
resentment（n.）憤慨、忿怒、怨恨

worker（n.）工人、勞工、勞動者
grandchildren（n.）孫子
receive（v.）收到、接到
education（n.）教育、培養、訓練
electrical（adj.）與電有關的、電氣科學的

Once he had been a farmer, but after his wound, he couldn't till his land. Fortunately, from the very beginning his wife had been good to him. No one in his family bore him any resentment.

I said that Uncle Zhang had two sons who became workers, but more than that, his grandchildren had all received good educations. In fact, one of them was an Electrical Engineering major at National Tsinghua University in Hsinzhu.

When the elderly Li heard this, he immediately became visibly excited. He said his sons were all farmers, but he had a grandson who would soon be a university student. "My grandson's smart as a whip and won himself a county scholarship," he went on. "That helped him go to a good middle school in the city, and now he's

engineering（n.）工程、工程學
major（n.）主修者
immediately（adv.）立即、即刻、馬上
visibly（adv.）明顯地
excite（v.）刺激、使興奮、使激動

grandson（n.）孫子、外孫
university（n.）大學、綜合性大學
whip（n.）鞭子
smart as a whip：非常聰明的
county（n.）縣
scholarship（n.）獎學金

入重點大學。現在是寒假期間，孫子放假，現在雖然不在家，但馬上就要回來了。

　　我總算看到了這個聰明的小子，他說他的分數應該可以進北京清華大學的電機系，我勸他萬一進不到清華，進入交大也相當好了。這位年輕人對我這位來自台灣的訪客極有興趣，他說他一輩子就只有一個願望，進入台積電裡面去參觀一下。他又透露了他的另一願望：聽張惠妹的歌。他告訴我他的宿舍裡有張惠妹的海報。

---

grade（n.）成績、評分
practice（n.）練習、實習、訓練
exam（n.）考試
quite（adv.）完全、徹底
first-rate（adj.）第一流的、最佳
的、最高級的
vacation（n.）休假、假期
measure（n.）打量、估量
fellow（n.）男人、傢伙、人
test（n.）測驗、小考

already in his third year there. He's gotten real high grades in his practice exams and I'm quite sure he'll get into a first-rate university. We're in the middle of the Chinese New Year break, so my grandson's on vacation. Although he's not here now, he'll soon be coming home."

After a while I was able to take my own measure of this smart young fellow. He told me his test scores could probably get him into the Electrical Engineering Department at National Thinghua University in Beijing. In the event his hopes for Thinghua did not work out, I encouraged him to try to get into National Jiaotong University. "That's also a fine school," I said.

This young man was keenly interested in this visitor who had come all the way from Taiwan. He said his

---

score（n.）（測驗的）成績、分數
probably（adv.）大概、或許、很可能
department（n.）（大學的）系、科系

encourage（v.）鼓勵、慫恿
keenly（adv.）敏銳地、銳利地、強烈地、熱心地
interest（v.）使感興趣

　　我臨機一動，將我的羽毛衣脫下來，送給了這位年輕人。我這件羽毛衣極為漂亮，是我太太買給我的，我太太很怕我有糟老頭子的模樣，所以經常替我買一些穿起來很帥的衣服，可惜我已白髮蒼蒼，再帥的衣服，穿在我的身上就不帥了。年輕人立刻穿上了這件羽毛衣，果真奇帥無比，他說將來一定要在清華園裡穿這件衣服照一張像。

---

semiconductor（n.）半導體
manufacturing（adj.）製造業的、製造的
company（n.）公司、商號

reveal（v.）揭示、揭露、暴露、洩露
poster（n.）海報
dormitory（n.）學生宿舍

whole life he had a hope. He hoped to visit the Taiwan Semiconductor Manufacturing Company and see what went on there. He revealed another dream. He wanted to hear A-mei sing in person. He said he had an A-mei poster over in his dormitory.

A moment of inspiration came to me. I wanted to slip out of the sweater I was wearing and give it to this young man. It was a beautiful sweater. My wife had bought it for me. My wife was always worrying about how I dressed, me, this old goat. So she was always picking up something "fashionable" for me. She wanted to make me fashionable! It was a pity my hair had already turned white. The latest in fashion trends didn't look fashionable at all on me.

The young fellow put the sweater on immediately. There was just no comparison. That sweater sure looked

---

inspiration（n.）靈感
slip（v.）匆忙地穿(或脫)
sweater（n.）毛線衣(厚)運動衫
fashionable（adj.）流行的、時尚

的、時髦的
pity（n.）可惜的事
trend（n.）趨勢、傾向
comparison（n.）比較、對照、類似

　　而我呢！脫下了羽毛衣，我忽然感到了一陣寒意。

李老先生看出了這點，他去屋裡找了一件棉襖送給了

我。

　　李老先生和我殷殷道別，他叫我轉告張伯伯多多保

重，也叫我問候張伯伯的家人，希望大家都能安居樂

業。

　　這件棉襖又跟著我飄洋過海，在飛機上，我卻獲得

了空中小姐的讚美，她說她從來沒有看到這麼帥的衣

---

campus（n.）校園、校區
hint（n.）少許、微量
chill（n.）風寒、寒顫
notice（v.）注意、察覺

farewell（n.）告別、告別辭
prosperity（n.）興旺、繁榮、昌盛、成功
ocean（n.）海洋、海

good on him. He said he'd be sure to wear it around the campus at Tsinghua. He'd get a picture of it too.

And as for me? Once I had taken the sweater off, I felt just a hint of a chill. The older Mr. Li noticed and went into the room for something. He came back and handed me a *mian au*.

The older Mr. Li and I finally said our farewells. He asked me to tell Uncle Zhang to take good care of himself. He wanted me to say hello to Uncle's family. He hoped everyone there would enjoy good health and prosperity.

That *mian au* flew over the ocean with me. It even drew compliments from one of the flight attendants. She

draw（v.）吸引、招來
compliment（n.）讚美的話、恭維、敬意

flight（n.）（飛機的）班次、（某班次的）飛機、班機
attendant（n.）服務員、侍者

服，還問我哪裡買的。

我見到了張伯伯，他很高興李少白現在生活得很好，但是他對於那位不知名的恩人心裡有無限的虧欠之情。我無法勸他看開一點，我沒有經歷過那一場可怕的戰爭，也許無法了解老兵的想法。

張伯伯在新竹清華大學念書的孫子正好來看爺爺，他一眼就看上了那件大陸鄉下人穿的棉襖，苦苦哀求我送他。我發現他穿了那件棉襖，的確很酷。看了這位台

claim（v.）自稱、聲稱、主張
eye-catching（adj.）引人注目的、顯著的
express（v.）表達、陳述、表示

endless（adj.）無盡的、長久的、不斷的、無休止的
affection（n.）愛、情愛、鍾愛
remorse（n.）痛悔、自責

claimed she had never seen a piece of clothing as eye-catching as that jacket, and wondered where I had bought it.

I saw Uncle Zhang. He was happy that Li Shaobai's life had taken such a happy turn. But he expressed his endless affection and thanks, but also remorse for his benefactor, a man whose name he would never know. I had no way to convince him to look at the positives in the situation. Well, I had never been caught in the thick of battle. Maybe it was just not possible to climb inside an old soldier's mind and know how he thought and felt.

Uncle Zhang's grandson who was studying in Hsinzhu at Tsinghua came home to visit his grandfather. He took one look at the *mian au* that had come from mainland China and begged me to give it to him. I made

---

benefactor（n.）捐助人、施主、恩人
convince（v.）使確信、使信服、說服
positive（n.）正面、光明面、樂觀面
situation（n.）處境、境遇
in the thick of：投入、置身於
beg（v.）請求、懇求

灣年輕人的樣子，我立刻想起了那位即將在大陸上大學的年輕人。

我真羨慕張伯伯和李老先生的兩個孫子，他們都有好的前程，他們如果相遇，一定是在非常愉快的場合。也許會在張惠妹的演唱會，也可能是在一個半導體的會議中；他們絕不會像他們爺爺們那樣，在寒冷的戰場上見面了。

——原載八十九年五月十一日《聯合副刊》

---

discovery（n.）被發現的事物
terrific（adj.）非常好的、了不起的
gaze（v.）凝視、注視
pop（v.）（意外地、突然地）出現、

發生、跳出
envy（v.）妒忌、羨慕
bright（adj.）光明的
future（n.）前途、未來

another discovery: He looked terrific in that jacket. As I gazed at this young Taiwanese youth, the image of that soon-to-be university student on the mainland popped into my mind.

I envied the two of them. I envied the grandson of Uncle Zhang and the grandson of the older Mr. Li as well. Those two had bright futures. What a happy place they would stand in if one day they could meet. Maybe it would happen at an A-mei concert or, possibly while they were exchanging scholarly research at an academic conference on semiconductors. Surely they wouldn't be like their grandfathers. They wouldn't be looking at each other on a desperately cold battlefield.

---

concert（n.）音樂會、演奏會
academic（adj.）學術的
conference（n.）會議、討論會、
協商會

desperately（adv.）絕望地、不顧
一切地、拼命地
battlefield（n.）戰場、戰地

窗 外
Outside the Window

康士林　譯

這位校長的食慾一下子就沒有了，他放下了叉子，也放下了快進口的一塊羊肉，小乞丐卻沒有離開，他聚精會神地注意那塊看上去美味無比的羊肉。

The President immediately lost his appetite, and put down his fork and withdrew the piece of lamb about to go into his mouth. The little beggar, however, did not leave and intently focused his attention on that most delectable piece of lamb that had been going into the President's mouth.

做校長，有一個好處，到別的大學去訪問，總會受到很好的接待。我最喜歡去的是一所英國大學，校長學的是精密機械，但好像極有修養，不但談話非常優雅，而且生活也很有品味。

他們學校的貴賓餐廳有片大型的落地玻璃窗，窗外有一大片草地，草永遠剪得很整齊，最好看的是草地中間的那棵大樹，那是蘋果樹。有一次，我春天去那裡，蘋果花盛開，校長請我吃飯的時候，坐在靠窗的桌子，一面用餐，一面欣賞窗外盛開的蘋果花，真是一種享受。

---

university president（n.）大學校長
precision mechanical engineering（n.）
精密機械工程
appear to 好像、似乎
cultivated（adj.）有教養的、文雅的
elegantly（adv.）優雅地
lifestyle（n.）生活風格、生活方式
standard（n.）標準、水準
guest dining hall（n.）貴賓餐廳

The one good thing about being a university president is that when you visit another university you will always be treated very well. I like best to go to a certain English university. The President studied precision mechanical engineering yet he appears to be very cultivated. Not only does he speak most elegantly, but his lifestyle has very high standards.

The guest dining hall of their university has large French windows. Outside the windows is a large lawn, which is always well-manicured. What is most attractive in the lawn is a very large trec, which is an apple tree. Once, when I went there in the spring, the apple tree was in full blossom. When the President invited me to eat, we sat at a table by the windows. As we were eating, we also enjoyed the apple tree in full blossom. It was really a kind of pleasure.

French window（n.）落地窗　　　apple tree（n.）蘋果樹
lawn（n.）草地、草坪　　　　　in full blossom 花盛開
well-manicured（adj.）整齊　　　enjoy（v.）欣賞、享受
attractive（adj.）吸引人的、嫵媚動　a kind of 一種
人的　　　　　　　　　　　　　pleasure（n.）愉快、樂趣

今年，我又去了，窗外仍然是賞心悅目的花園，蘋果花也盛開，可是那靠窗的桌子不見了，我們在裡面的一張桌子吃飯，校長本人吃得極為簡單，其他人也如此，好像大家都在吃麵包和湯。我向來痛恨洋人的牛排，吃簡單的食物我十分快樂。

可是我心中總有點納悶，為什麼靠窗的桌子不見了？為什麼大家吃得如此簡單？校長顯然看出了我的困惑，他告訴了我到底發生了什麼事。

有一天，這位校長到印度的加爾各答去開會，他在

---

delightfully（adv.）令人愉悅地　　no longer 不再
beautiful（adj.）美麗、漂亮　　further（adj.）較遠的
garden（n.）花園、庭園　　within（prep.）在…裡面
gorgeous（adj.）美麗、燦爛　　sparingly（adv.）節儉、簡樸

This year I again went to that English university. Outside the windows was still the delightfully beautiful garden, and the apple blossoms were gorgeous, but there was no longer that table near the window. We ate at a table further within the room, and president ate very sparingly as did the others at the table. Everyone was having bread and soup. I have always hated with a passion the steaks of foreigners, so to eat simple food made me a hundred-percent happy.

Yet I still was a little troubled. Why was the table by the windows not to be seen? Why was everyone eating so simply? The President saw my confusion and told me what had happened.

One day, this President went to Kolkata in India for a meeting. As he was walking in the city, he saw a

---

bread (n.) 麵包
soup (n.) 湯
passion (n.) 激動、激情
steak (n.) 牛排
foreigner (n.) 外國人

hundred-percent 百分之百
troubled (adj.) 困惑、納悶
confusion (n.) 疑惑、困惑
meeting (n.) 開會、會議

街上散步的時候，看到一間餐館，這間餐館有一大片落

地的玻璃窗，靠窗有好幾張桌子，每張桌子都鋪了雪白

的桌布，桌布上放了雪亮的銀器，瓷器一望即知來自英

國，講究之至。校長毫不猶豫地走了進去，選了一張靠

窗的桌子坐下。這家餐館不但布置得好，菜也燒得好，

這位校長覺得這一切都十全十美，他還記得當時他點的

菜是蔥燒羊腿。

　　就在他津津有味地品嘗那塊羊腿的時候，他忽然發

現窗外有一個小乞丐目不轉睛地看他。這個小男孩上身

沒有穿衣服，他對那塊羊腿全神貫注地看著，由於他想

restaurant（n.）餐廳、餐館	silverware（n.）銀器
nearby（adj.）附近	dishware（n.）餐具
spread（v.）鋪有、擺有	proper（adj.）適當的、高尚的
sparkling-white（adj.）雪白、亮白	a bit of 一點
table cloth（n.）桌巾	hesitancy（n.）猶豫、遲疑
gleaming（adj.）閃閃發光的、雪亮的	select（v.）選擇、挑選

restaurant that. had French windows with a number of tables nearby. On each table was spread a sparkling-white table cloth, upon which were gleaming silverware and dishware. One look and you knew it was all from England and most proper.

Without a bit of hesitancy, the President entered and selected a table by the windows. This restaurant was not only well-appointed but the cuisine was also good. The President felt that everything left nothing to be desired. He still remembered that he had ordered lamb chops and onions.

Just as the President was tasting that delicious lamb chop, he suddenly discovered outside the window a little beggar intently staring at him.

---

well-appointed（adj.）設備完善的
cuisine（n.）烹調、菜色
desired（adj.）需求、想要
order（v.）點菜、定購
lamb chop（n.）羊腿肉、羊排
onion（n.）洋蔥

taste（v.）品嘗
delicious（adj.）美味的、好吃的
discover（v.）發現
beggar（n.）乞丐、乞討者
intently（adv.）專注地、專心地
stare at 凝視、盯著看

看得很清楚，他的鼻子完全貼在窗戶上，兩隻手掌也是

完全放在窗上。

　　這位校長的食慾一下子就沒有了，他放下了叉子，

也放下了快進口的一塊羊肉，小乞丐卻沒有離開，他聚

精會神地注意那塊看上去美味無比的羊肉。

　　在印度很多餐館都有警衛的，就在這個時候，那位

警衛走了過來，小乞丐一溜煙地跑掉了。校長跑出去追

他，他卻已無影無蹤。校長回餐館以後，唯一做的事情

---

waist（n.）上身、腰部
concentration（n.）全神貫注、專心
stick to 黏住、貼著
grasp（v.）抓住、抓牢

immediately（adv.）立刻、馬上
appetite（n.）胃口
fork（n.）叉子
withdraw（v）收回

The little boy was not wearing anything above his waist and with full concentration was looking at the lamb chop. Because he wanted to see it a bit better, he had his nose stuck to the window. His hands were also grasping the window.

The President immediately lost his appetite, and put down his fork and withdrew the piece of lamb about to go into his mouth. The little beggar, however, did not leave and intently focused his attention on that most delectable piece of lamb that had been going into the President's mouth.

Many restaurants in India have guards. Just at that moment, the guard came over and the little beggar ran off in a flash. The President ran out to follow him, but the little beggar had left no trace. After the President had returned to the restaurant, the only thing he did was to

leave（v.）離開
focus（v.）聚焦、集中
attention（n.）注意力
delectable（adj.）好吃的、味美的
guard（n.）警衛

come over 過來、跑來
ran off 跑走
in a flash 剎那間、立刻
trace（n.）蹤影、蹤跡

是付了帳，他沒有吃完那頓飯。

　　以後，每次他坐在窗前吃飯，一定會想到那位小乞丐。不僅如此，每當他吃講究食物的時候，他就會感到有一個飢餓的小乞丐在看他吃。從此以後，他不再去使用那張放在貴賓室窗下的桌子，他的故事慢慢地傳了出去，全校很少有人去用那張桌子了。最後，貴賓室的負責人索性將那張窗前的桌子拿走了。校長也不再吃講究的食物，因為他不願感到有飢餓的小孩子在看他，他顯然影響了那所大學的很多教授，大家越吃越簡單了。

---

pay the bill 付帳、付錢
finish（v.）吃完
meal（n.）一餐、一頓
afterwards（adv.）後來、然後
whenever（conj.）不論何時、每當

definitely（adv.）一定、肯定
exquisite（adj.）精緻、講究
hungry（adj.）飢餓
slowly（adv.）慢慢地
circulate（v.）流傳、傳播

pay the bill. He did not finish his meal.

Afterwards, whenever the President had a meal near a window, he definitely thought of that little beggar. And this was not all. Whenever he had something exquisite to eat, he would always feel that there was a hungry little beggar looking at him. Afterwards, he did not again use the table by the windows in the guest dining room. His story slowly was circulated and hardly anyone in the school ever used that table. Finally, the manager of the guest dining room just removed the table from in front of the windows. The President did not continue to eat any exquisite food, because he did not want to experience a hungry child looking at him. Obviously the President had influenced many of the faculty of that university. Everyone ate more simply.

---

hardly（adv.）幾乎不、幾乎沒有
finally（adv.）最後、終於
manager（n.）負責人、經理
remove（v.）搬開、移走
in front of 在…之前
continue（v.）繼續

experience（v.）經歷、感受
obviously（adv.）顯然、明顯
influence（v.）影響
faculty（n.）教職員
simply（adv.）簡單、簡樸

在回程的飛機上，我發現飛機上的食物相當講究，我突發奇想，問服務生我可不可以吃一種簡單的食物，她毫無困難地答應了。她給我很多好吃的麵包和一盤湯，還有一些沙拉。

她告訴我，最近好多人要吃這種簡單的食物，因此航空公司索性想出了這種簡餐，她問我為什麼最近這麼多人要吃簡餐，我沒有回答。如果我說，窗外有飢餓的小孩在看我們吃東西，她大概不會懂的。

——原載《聯合副刊》

flight（n.）飛行、航程
suddenly（adv.）突然、忽然
strike（v.）打動、閃現
thought（n.）想法
attendant（n.）服務員

flight attendant 空服員
agree（v.）同意、答應
problem（n.）困難、問題
good tasting 好吃的、美味的

On the flight back to Taiwan, I discovered that the food on the plane was rather special. Suddenly I was struck by a strange thought, and asked the flight attendant if I could have something simple. She agreed saying that it would be not a problem. She gave me many good tasting rolls and some ordinary soup. Also some salad.

She told me that recently many people wanted to eat more simply, so the company just came up with this simple meal. She asked me why so many people recently want to cat simply. I did not reply. If I had said that a beggar child would be looking at me from outside the window, she would probably not have understood.

---

roll（n.）麵包捲、捲餅
ordinary（adj.）普通、一般
salad（n.）沙拉
recently（adv.）最近、近來
company（n.）公司

reply（v.）回答、答覆
probably（adv.）也許、大概
understand（v.）了解、明白

命 好
Good Fate

鮑端磊　譯

　　我終於懂得什麼叫「命好」了，「命好」就是小的時候，只碰到了好人，沒有碰到壞人。

　　I finally understand what it means to have "a good fate". If you are blessed with a good fate, that means that when you are young, you meet good people, and not bad people.

　　王胖子是我的好友，我認識他是因為我教他的兒子彈鋼琴。有一天，琴練好了，我要離開的時候，聞到一陣菜香，忍不住向廚房張望，發現王胖子滿頭大汗地在燒菜。他看到我的饞相，留我待下來吃午飯，他告訴我他是台中市一家四星級大飯店的主廚。

　　我太太知道王胖子是大飯店的主廚以後，立刻下令要我用一切方法和王胖子建立友誼。王胖子知道我們夫婦好吃的弱點，就壓迫我陪他打網球，他這個胖子燒飯技術一流，打網球卻不入流，沒有什麼人會想陪他打網球，我為了想吃他燒的菜，只好經常陪他打；他也沒有

fatty（n.）胖子
capacity（n.）資格、身分
aroma（n.）香味
catch（v.）吸引、引起
attention（n.）注意
resist（v.）忍耐、忍住

take a peek 張望、窺視
drench（v.）濕透、浸濕
cook up a storm 很努力地作菜
expression（n.）臉色、表現
master chef（n.）主廚
order（v.）命令、指示

Fatty Wang is my good friend. I met him in my capacity as a piano teacher for his son. One day after our lesson had ended, I was all ready to leave when the aroma of food caught my attention. I just couldn't resist taking a peek in the kitchen. There I found Fatty Wang, drenched in sweat, cooking up a storm. He saw the expression on my face and asked me to stay for lunch. He told me he was a master chef at a four star hotel in Taichung.

After my wife found out Fatty Wang was a master chef at a big hotel, she ordered me to come up with a way to establish a friendship with him. Well, Fatty Wang knew our couple's weakness for fine cuisine. He put all kinds of pressure on me to become his tennis partner.

Now, this heavy-set fellow might have had a knack

---

come up with 想出
establish（v.）建立
friendship（n.）友誼
couple（n.）夫婦
weakness（n.）弱點、愛好

cuisine（n.）廚藝、菜餚
pressure（n.）壓力、迫使
partner（n.）拍檔、伙伴
heavy-set（adj.）胖的、粗壯的
knack（n.）特殊本領、熟練技巧

使我失望，經常做幾道菜，邀我們兩口子帶唯一的女兒去吃飯。

　　王胖子是個大好人，他告訴我他還有一個兼職，在彰化的少年輔育院教那裡的一些孩子燒飯。王胖子收入奇高，這是公開的祕密，他去那裡兼職，其實是等於做義工，很多過去有前科的孩子們，離開輔育院以後都找到了餐飲業的工作，其中王胖子有很大的功勞。

---

possibly（adv.）也許、可能
play tennis 打網球
hook（v.）謀得
disappoint（v.）使失望、使沮喪
whip up 迅速做好（飯菜）

along（adv.）一起、帶著
truly（adv.）真的、的確
juvenile（adj.）青少年的
detention center（n.）拘留所、輔育院

for cooking. But he sure didn't have a knack for tennis. No one could possibly come up with the idea of playing tennis with that guy. But, well, the only way to hook a chance to eat his cooking was to be his tennis partner. And he didn't disappoint me, either. He'd whip up a few dishes and invite us over to eat. "Bring that little girl of yours along too," he'd say.

Fatty Wang is truly a good man. He told me he had a second job. He taught a cooking class for the Juvenile Detention Center in Changhua. It was more or less a public secret that Fatty Wang made good moncy. Going over there for that second job of his was practically like being a volunteer to help others. Over the years, many a young person with a rough and tumble past left that center able to find good work in the food and hospitality industry. Fatty Wang should be given credit for that.

---

more or less 或多或少、有點
public secret（n.）公開祕密
practically（adv.）其實、實際上
volunteer（n.）義工、志工
rough and tumble（adj.）混亂的、

激烈的
hospitality（n.）好客、款待
industry（n.）行業、工業
credit（n.）功勞、榮譽

　　有一天，打完網球以後，王胖子告訴我，他在輔育院發現了一個孩子，頗有音樂天才，他說我應該進去以義工身分指導他。

　　這個孩子叫做趙松村，他的確有音樂天分，他完全無師自通地會彈鋼琴和吹長笛，我的任務只是糾正他的一些錯誤而已。我說他有音樂天分，是指他的音感特別好，只要有人唱一首歌，他立刻就能在鋼琴上彈出來，右手彈的是主旋律，左手彈的是伴奏，伴奏通常是他自己隨興編的。這種學生，真是打了燈籠都找不到。

---

match（n.）比賽　　　　　　piano（n.）鋼琴
gift（n.）天賦、才能　　　　flute（n.）長笛
no doubt 無疑、的確　　　　simply（adv.）只是、僅僅
talent（n.）天才、才華　　　straighten out（v.）改正、糾正
benefit（n.）好處、利益　　　minor（adj.）較小的、次要的

One day after a tennis match, Fatty Wang said he had found a child at the center who had a special gift for music. He told me I ought to go over there and volunteer my services. "Give the boy a hand," he said.

The name of the child was Zhao Songcun, and there was no doubt about his musical talent. He never had the benefit of a teacher, and had taught himself to play both the piano and the flute. My job was simply to straighten out a few minor wrinkles. I said he had musical talent. What I mean is the boy had an inspiration for music. Let someone sing a song, and he'd sit right down at a piano and tap it out. His right hand would play the melody and his left hand accompany. Usually the accompaniment was a little ditty he thought up right there on the spot. You could search a valley of darkness

---

wrinkle（n.）小缺點、問題
inspiration（n.）靈感
tap out 敲打出、彈出
melody（n.）旋律、主調
accompany（v.）伴奏

accompaniment（n.）伴奏
ditty（n.）小調、小曲子
search（v.）尋找、搜尋
valley（n.）山谷、溪谷
darkness（n.）黑暗、陰暗

　　趙松村和我學了一陣子音樂以後，開始告訴我他的

身世。他的父親在他小時候就中了風，成了植物人，可

是一直活著，住在一家醫院裡。他從小靠他母親帶他長

大，因為他們的家在非常偏遠的鄉下，沒有什麼工作可

找，母親只好打零工來掙生活費。在他念國一的時候，

好幾次沒有錢買鞋子，常常赤腳上學，書錢也交不起，

都是老師們幫他解決的。他本來也不喜歡念書，這種念

書生涯，使他感到厭倦，決定一走了之，到台北去打天

下，當時他才只是國中二年級的學生。

---

massive（adj.）巨大的、大量的
spotlight（n.）聚光燈
suffer（v.）受苦、患病、罹患
stroke（n.）中風
coma（n.）昏迷

alive（adj.）活著
unconscious（adj.）不醒人事的、
失去知覺的
childhood（n.）兒時、童年
depend on 依靠、依賴

with a massive spotlight and never find a student like that.

After Zhao Songcun and I studied a bit of music, he began to tell me his life story.

His father suffered a stroke when the boy was very young and then went into a coma. His father was still alive, but lay flat on his back in a hospital, completely unconscious. From his childhood Songcun depended only on his mother, but because their family lived far out in the countryside, there just wasn't any work to be found. His mother could only get low-paying odd jobs. When he was in first year of junior high school, many a time he didn't have the money to buy shoes. Often he went to school in his bare feet. There was no money for books. That was a problem his teachers had to solve for him. In the beginning he just didn't like anything related

---

countryside（n.）鄉下、農村
low-paying（adj.）低薪
odd job（n.）臨時工作、零工
many a time 多次、常常

bare feet（n.）打赤腳
solve（v.）解決
in the beginning 起初、一開始
related to 與…有關

　　他在一家營造商那裡找到了一份苦工的工作，雖然累，收入卻使得他感到好快活，他還寄錢回去給他媽媽。沒有想到的是他媽媽出了一次車禍，他趕回去的時候，他母親已經斷了氣。他從他媽媽的遺物中，拿了一條十字架項鍊作為紀念，也從此變成了無依無靠的孤兒。他雖然有一個阿姨，阿姨家境也不好，無法照顧他，因此他回到了台北。

---

sort（n.）種類、類型
hardscrabble（adj.）艱辛困苦的
miserable（adj.）悲慘、可憐
take off 啟程
sophomore（n.）二年級學生

back-breaking（adj.）苦工、辛苦的
construction（n.）建築、營建
exhausted（adj.）精疲力盡
imagine（v.）猜想、料想
automobile accident（n.）車禍

to school or books. The sort of hardscrabble study life he knew only made him miserable. He decided he'd go away, take off for Taipei and find whatever work he could. At that time he was a sophomore in high school.

He found a back-breaking job in construction. It may have left him exhausted, but the money he made helped him feel alive. At that time he was still sending money back to his mother. He never imagined his mother might get into an automobile accident. He was still rushing back home when she breathed her last. From his mother's belongings he took a chain with a crucifix on it, something to remember her by. From that moment on, he was an orphan without anyone to lean on. Although he did have an auntie, the auntie's family had troubles of its own. They had no way to take care of him, and so he went back to Taipei.

---

rush（v.）趕、奔
breathe（v.）呼吸
belongings（n.）所有物、財產
chain（n.）項鍊
crucifix（n.）十字架

orphan（n.）孤兒
lean on 依靠
auntie（n.）阿姨、伯母、嬸嬸、舅媽
take care of 照顧、照料

　　趙松村慢慢地感到做建築工人太苦了，雖然薪水不錯，可是成天在大太陽下流汗，幾乎沒有一分鐘身子不是臭臭的。他羨慕那些在KTV裡服務的孩子們，他們可以穿襯衫，有的還打領結，又不要曬太陽。雖然薪水不高，至少好像有點社會地位，所以他就設法改行，做了一名KTV的服務生。

　　當初在做工人的時候，他從來沒有交過壞朋友，現在不同了，他交了一大堆壞朋友。究竟他犯了什麼錯，我不便說，我只能說，他犯的錯全是他的那些壞朋友教出來的。

---

gradually（adv.）慢慢地、逐漸地
harsh（adj.）辛苦、苛刻
scalding（adj.）炙熱的
stink（v.）發臭
envy（v.）羨慕

tie（n.）領帶、領結
fry（v.）油炸、受日曬的煎熬
salary（n.）薪水
at least 至少
social position（n.）社會地位

Zhao Songcun gradually came to feel that construction work was simply too harsh. Although the money wasn't bad, it meant sweating all day long under a scalding sun, and in the end there wasn't a single minute your body wasn't stinking. He envied young people who had service jobs in KTVs. They could wear a shirt, and some of them a tie too. They didn't have to fry under the sun. Although the salary was not high, at least there seemed to be a bit of a social position in it. So he managed to step up and become a student-aged worker at a KTV.

When he had labored earlier as a construction worker, Songcun had never dealt with so called "bad influences" among his friends. It was different now. He now was making friends with all sorts of negative elements in society. Naturally it's a bit embarrassing for me to mention the kind of slips he got himself into. I can

---

step up 提昇、向前跨出一大步
labor（v.）工作、勞動
dealt with 處理、應付
bad influence（n.）壞影響、損友
negative（adj.）負面的、不好的

elements（n.）一群人
embarrassing（adj.）令人為難、尷尬的
mention（v.）提及、說起
slip（n.）錯誤

他非常關心他爸爸，他說他過去過一陣子就會去看看他爸爸，現在不行了。我找了一個週末，去桃園那家醫院看了他爸爸，也回來告訴他，他爸爸仍是老樣子，他可以放心。

趙松村又告訴我，他有一個小弟弟，他離開家的時候，小弟弟四歲，他回去替媽媽下葬的時候，小弟弟被好心的人送走了，當時小弟弟只有五歲，他的小弟弟叫做趙松川，現在在台中一所國小念五年級，他又求我去看看他唯一的小弟弟。他一再地告訴我，他弟弟命比他好。

---

misstep（n.）錯誤、過失　　　　bury（v.）埋葬、安葬
worry（n.）憂慮、擔心　　　　good-hearted（adj.）好心的、仁慈的

only say that whatever missteps he did make, well, they were all because of the bad influence of his friends.

He had always taken very good care of his father. He said that in the past he often went to see his father. Now at the center there was nothing he could do about that. I found a weekend and went to his father's hospital in Taoyuan. I saw Songcun's father and came back and told him he was the same. He could put his worries to rest.

Zhao Songcun told me that he had a younger brother. When he left home, the little guy was four years old. When he went back to bury his mother, his little brother was under the care of some good-hearted people. The brother was five years old at that time. He was called Zhao Songchuan and was now in the fifth grade at an elementary school in Taichung. Songcun also asked me to go visit his one and only little brother. Again and again he said his brother's fate was better than his.

elementary school (n.) 小學   fate (n.) 命運

我們做老師的人，很容易進入國小，我找到了小弟弟趙松川的導師，他說趙松川正在從操場裡走回來，在一大堆蹦蹦跳跳的小鬼中間，他指出了趙松川。趙松川顯然是個快樂而又胡鬧的小男孩，他一身大汗，一面擦汗，一面和他的同學打鬧。

我想到了趙松村，他一直有點憂鬱感，很少露出快樂的笑容，尤其吹長笛的時候，總是將一首歌吹得如泣如訴。而現在看到弟弟趙松川，卻是如此一個快樂的孩子。

profession（n.）職業	midst（n.）中間、中央
easily（adv.）容易	a throng of 一群
track down 找到	fry（n.）成群的孩子
guidance（n.）指導、輔導	dash（v.）急衝、奔跑
counselor（n.）指導老師、導師	clearly（adv.）顯然
athletic field（n.）操場	rambunctious（adj.）喧鬧、胡鬧
point out 指出	

We in the teaching profession can get into an elementary school quite easily, and there I tracked down Zhao Songchuan's guidance counselor. He said Songchuan was just coming in from the athletic field. He pointed him out to me in the midst of a throng of small fries, all dashing and jumping around. Clearly, Zhao Songchuan was a happy, rambunctious little boy, covered with perspiration one moment and wiping himself dry the other. He was having a fun and noisy time of it with his classmates.

I pictured Zhao Songcun in my mind. He always had a touch of melancholy about him and rarely flashed any sign of a smile. That was particularly true when he played the flute. His songs seemed to be tunes filled with lament and tears. Now here I was looking at his lit-

---

perspiration（n.）汗水
wipe（v.）擦拭、擦淨
noisy（adj.）嘈雜的、喧鬧的
classmate（n.）同學
picture（v.）想像、想到
a touch of 一點、少許

melancholy（n.）憂鬱、鬱悶
rarely（adv.）很少
flash（v.）閃現、露出
particularly（adv.）特別、尤其
tune（n.）歌曲、曲調
lament（n.）哀悼、痛哭

　　導師告訴我，趙松川一向快樂，人緣也好。我問他是不是他被一個好家庭領養了？導師的回答令我吃了一驚，他說他五歲就進了一家孤兒院，一直住在孤兒院裡。

　　我的好奇心使我當天晚上就去了這家孤兒院。孤兒院的院長是位年輕的牧師，他帶我參觀了孤兒院，也告訴我他們了解趙松川的哥哥現在被關了，他們發現趙松川根本不記得有這麼一個哥哥，他們打算暫時不告訴他，等他大了以後才告訴他。

---

obviously（adv.）明顯、顯然
happy-go-lucky 無憂無慮、隨遇而安

get along with 相處融洽
raise（v.）扶養、養育
astonished（adj.）驚訝、訝異

tle brother Sung-chuan, who was quite obviously a very, very happy child.

His counselor told me Zhao Songchuan was a happy-go-lucky type. He got along well with everyone around him. I asked, "Isn't a kind family raising him?" I was astonished when he said he had entered an orphanage at the age of five. He had lived there ever since.

My curiosity led me to that orphanage that very night. The director of the place was a young minister. He led me around the orphanage. He said they understood that Songchuan's older brother was locked up. They had discovered that Zhao Songchuan had absolutely no memory of any older brother. The plan for now was not to tell him. They would wait until he was older and then break the news to him.

---

orphanage（n.）孤兒院　　　　lock up 關起、鎖起
curiosity（n.）好奇心　　　　absolutely（adv.）絕對、完全
minister（n.）牧師、神職人員　　break the news 透露消息

　　孤兒院並不是經費非常充裕的地方，可是孩子們快樂卻是十分明顯，我常常發現孩子要我抱他，他們好像認為陌生人都是好人。

　　牧師告訴我，當天晚上有一個晚禱，孩子們都要參加的，我應邀而往。晚禱很短，結束的時候，大家一起唱〈你愛不愛我〉，我從來沒有聽過這首歌，可是一學就會了。這首歌的第一段是獨唱，由趙松川唱的，原來他和他大哥一樣，極有音樂天才。晚禱完了以後，我正要離開，趙松川跑過來，要我彎下身來親親他。牧師告訴我，這是他的習慣，喜歡叫陌生人親親他。

---

wealthy（adj.）充裕、富裕　　prayer（n.）祈禱、禱告
institute（n.）機構　　　　　attend（v.）參加
hug（n.）擁抱　　　　　　　　brief（adj.）簡短
stranger（n.）陌生人　　　　　conclude（v.）結束

That orphanage surely was not a wealthy institute, but it was very obvious the children there were happy. I often find that children want a hug from me. It seems they feel strangers are good people.

The minister said they had an evening prayer service that evening. The children would all attend it, and I was welcome to stay. The evening prayer was quite brief. As it concluded, everyone sang the hymn "Do You Love Me or Not?" I had never heard that song, but quickly got the gist of it. The first stanza was sung solo by Zhao Songchuan. It was just like that: He and his older brother were alike that way. They both had a gift for music.

After the evening prayer service ended, I was just getting ready to go, and Zhao Songchuan ran up to me.

---

hymn（n.）讚歌、聖歌
gist（n.）要點、主旨
stanza（n.）詩節（歌詞或詩的一段）

solo（adv.）獨唱
alike（adj.）相像的
run up to 跑向

　　我將我的所見所聞一五一十地告訴了趙松村。他聽了以後，告訴我他去看過他的弟弟，第一次見面，是一個星期天，他的弟弟穿了白襯衫、白長褲，打了一個紅領結，站在教堂的唱詩班裡，當時他就不敢去認他弟弟了。第二次，他又悄悄地去造訪孤兒院，這次發現，他弟弟在打電腦，他發現他弟弟不但會用電腦，還會英文，而他呢？他一輩子沒有碰過電腦，英文單字本來就沒有記得幾個，現在是一個也記不得了。

---

share（v.）分享　　　　　　ensconced（adj.）安置
deck out 穿著、打扮　　　　choir（n.）唱詩班

He wanted me to turn around and give him a kiss. The minister explained that was what he always did. He liked to tell strangers to give him a kiss.

I shared the whole story from A to Z with Zhao Songcun. I told him everything I had seen and heard. After he heard my story, he said he had gone to visit his little brother. The first time for them to see one another at the orphanage was on a Sunday. His brother was all decked out in a white shirt and white pants. He had a red tie around his neck and was ensconced in the choir. He didn't dare tell his little brother who he was.

The second time too he snuck in as a visitor and this time he discovered his brother knew how to use a computer. Not only did he find his brother used a computer, but he was also good at English. And what about Songcun? He had never even touched a computer. And as for English, he never could remember more than the

---

dare（v.）敢、膽敢　　　　　computer（n.）電腦
sneak in 溜進去

　　當他開始交上壞朋友以後，他就沒有再去看他的弟弟，他知道弟弟並不認識他。他雖然覺得和那些朋友一起出去玩，是一件很爽的事，可是他不希望他弟弟知道有這麼一個哥哥。

　　在我們開始練琴以前，趙松村又說了，「李老師，我不是說過嗎？我弟弟命比我好。如果我小時候就進入了孤兒院，今天我就不會在這裡了。」

　　聖誕節到了，今年，輔育院請孤兒院的孩子們來共同舉辦聯歡晚會，我和王胖子也參加了。各種的表演過

vocabulary（n.）單字、字彙　　　recognize（v.）認出、認識
recall（v.）回想、想起　　　　　rush（n.）快感

simplest vocabulary. Now he couldn't recall a single word.

Once he had gotten in with those bad elements among his friends, he had just never gone back to see his younger brother. He knew his brother wouldn't recognize him. He felt going out for good times with that bad bunch of his gave him a happy rush, but deep in his heart he hoped his little brother never found out he had a brother like him.

When we first began his piano lessons, Zhao Songcun said to me, "Professor Lee, didn't I already tell you? My little brother's fate is better than mine. If I could have gone into an orphanage when I was a boy, I wouldn't be here now."

At Christmas time this year, the Juvenile Detention Center invited the children from the orphanage to partic-

---

Christmas（n.）耶誕節　　　　participate（v.）參加、參與

後，壓軸是大合唱〈你愛不愛我〉，在台上，首先由輔

育院的趙松村演奏長笛，這次他沒有將這首歌吹成傷感

的調子。接著是獨唱，而獨唱的居然是他的弟弟趙松

川，在場只有我、王胖子和哥哥趙松村知道他們是兄

弟，獨唱完了，大家一起站起來合唱。我注意到趙松村

在弟弟獨唱的時候，眼淚已經流出來了。大家合唱的時

候，他沒有唱，一直在擦眼淚。

　　合唱完了以後，弟弟趙松川又跑到他哥哥那裡，他

天真爛漫地說：「大哥哥，你的長笛吹得好好聽，應該

親親我。」趙松村彎下身來親親他，他忽然從他頸子上

拿下了那個媽媽留給他的十字架項鍊，掛在他弟弟的身

---

program（n.）節目　　　　　　masterful（adj.）出色的
performance（n.）表演、演奏　　rendition（n.）表演、演奏
grand finale（n.）壓軸　　　　　audience（n.）觀眾

ipate in a music program. Fatty Wang and I attended it together. After all sorts of performances the grand finale was a masterful rendition of "Do You Love Me or Not?" First on stage was Zhao Songcun of the Center playing the flute. This time the rendition he offered the audience wasn't sorrowful at all. This was followed by a solo performance, and the soloist, of course, turned out to be his younger brother Zhao Songchuan. The only people in that hall who knew they were brothers were myself, Fatty Wang, and the older brother Songcun.

When the solo segment came to an end, everyone stood and sang the hymn together. I had kept an eye on Zhao Songcun when his brother sang that solo of his, and tears ran down his face. When the audience sang the hymn, Songcun didn't sing a word. He just dabbed his tears away.

---

sorrowful（adj.）傷感的、悲傷的　　segment（n.）部分、分段
soloist（n.）獨唱者　　　　　　　　dab（v.）輕擦
hall（n.）大廳、會堂

上。他弟弟被這個動作愣住了，可是仍然大方地謝謝他

的哥哥，走下台來。

　　這次，我和王胖子有點忍不住了。在回家的路上，

王胖子對我說：「我終於懂得什麼叫『命好』了，『命

好』就是小的時候，只碰到了好人，沒有碰到壞人。我

小的時候，沒有錢念一般高中，而要去念高職，也無法

---

innocently（adv.）天真無邪地　　plant（v.）放置
terrific（adj.）非常好、了不起　　abruptly（adv.）突然
spin around 原地打轉　　flummoxed（adj.）困惑、愣住

When the singing ended, the younger brother Zhao Songchuan ran over to his big brother. "Big Brother, " he said innocently, "you were terrific on that flute. You should give me a kiss."

Zhao Songcun spun around and planted a kiss on him. Then, abruptly, the older brother took the cross and chain from his neck and put it on his little brother. The little brother seemed flummoxed by the move, but recovered and thanked his brother profusely before dashing off the stage.

At this, Fatty Wang and I could hardly restrain ourselves.

On the drive home, Fatty said to me, "I finally understand what it means to have 'a good fate'. If you are blessed with a good fate, that means that when you are young, you meet good people, and not bad people.

---

recover（v.）恢復
profusely（adv.）大方、不吝惜地
dash off 迅速離去

hardly（adv.）幾乎不
restrain（v.）抑制、遏止
bless（v.）祝福、賜福

念大學，可是我一直沒有碰到壞人，如果我小的時候就

碰到壞人，我一定也會學壞的。」

　　我說：「王胖子，你說得有道理，可是命仍然可以

改的，如果我們這些好人多和他們做朋友，他們就不會

變壞了。」

　　王胖子同意我的說法，他說看起來，趙松村的命已

經改過來了。雖然外面很冷，我們仍然感到溫暖。

---

vocational（adj.）職業的
crowd（n.）大眾、人群、一群人

wind up 以…作結、結果是…
louse（n.）卑鄙的傢伙、壞人

When I was young, I didn't have the money to go to middle school and I wanted to go to a vocational high school. There was no way for me to ever attend a university. But I sure never met any bad people. If I had gotten in with a bad crowd when I was a kid, I'm sure I'd have wound up a louse."

"Fatty Wang, " I replied, "that's the truth. But people can still change their fate. What it takes is for we who are good to make friends with them more often. Then they can't turn bad."

Fatty Wang agreed with my words. He said it seemed as if Zhao Songcun's fate had already begun to change.

Although it was chilly outside, we were feeling pretty warm inside.

---

reply （v.）回答
agree with 同意

chilly （adj.）寒冷

　　附註：〈你愛不愛我〉，可以在《輕歌讚主榮》三

一七頁找到。

　　　　——原載八十七年十一月十一日《聯合報》〈微風細雨集〉

Note: Readers can find the hymn "Do You Love Me or Not?" on page 317 of the hymnal "Qng Ge Zan Zu Rong."

吳教授的慾望
The Desire of Professor Wu

康士林　譯

　　小男孩並沒有覺察到吳教授的表情，他緊緊地抱住吳教授，將他的頭靠在吳教授的肩膀上，一副舒適而滿足的模樣。

　　The little boy did not experience Professor Wu's uncomfortableness, and tightly hugged him, placing his head near Professor Wu's shoulders in a most relaxed and satisfied fashion.

吳教授是一位非常討人喜歡的人，他老是笑臉迎人，也很少講令人不愉快的話。可是我注意到他最近有時忽然會有一種不舒服的表情，只是這種表情很快地就會消失。

我第一次注意到他這種表情，是我們開院務會議的時候，吳教授坐在我的對面，當時院長在長篇大論地訓話，忽然吳教授表現出很不舒服，雖然只有一下子，但我注意到了。另外一次，我和吳教授打網球，打完網球，往停車場走過去的時候，他那種表情又出現了。

professor（n.）教授
attract（v.）吸引、引起注意
welcome（v.）歡迎
rarely（adv.）很少、難得
cause（v.）引起、招致
unhappy（adj.）不快樂、不舒服
recently（adv.）最近、近來

detect（v.）發現、察覺
all of a sudden 突然、一下子
look（v.）看起來
uncomfortable（adj.）不舒服、不自在
quickly（adv.）很快地、立刻
disappear（v.）消失、不見

Professor Wu is a person who attracts other people to him. He always welcomes others with a smile and rarely says anything to cause the other person to be unhappy. But recently I've detected that sometimes all of a sudden he looks uncomfortable but this look quickly disappears.

The first time I noticed his uncomfortable look was when we were holding a College Faculty Council. Professor Wu was sitting opposite to me. As the Dean of our College was reprimanding us in a long sermon, Professor Wu suddenly had a look of uncomfortableness. Even though it was just for a second, I noticed it. Another time was when Professor Wu and I had just finished playing tennis. As we were walking to the parking

---

notice（v.）注意、察覺
hold（v.）舉行、開會
College Faculty Council（n.）院務會議
opposite to 在…對面
dean（n.）學院院長、大學教務長
reprimand（v.）訓示、斥責

sermon（n.）冗長訓示
suddenly（adv.）突然、忽然
uncomfortableness（n.）不舒服
even though 即使、雖然
finish（v.）結束、完成
play tennis 打網球
parking lot（n.）停車場

　　這次，我直截了當地問吳教授是怎麼一回事，他告訴我他有差不多兩年的時間，會忽然感到頭痛，他去看過各種醫生，也做過各式各樣的檢查，一點兒毛病也查不出來。吳教授知道他這種毛病一定很難查出病因，因為他到醫院去的時候，總是好好地，醫生如何能查出病因呢？我問他會不會晚上睡覺的時候被頭痛弄醒，他說不會，我又問他會不會在運動的時候感到頭痛，他說好像也不會。吳教授曾經是少棒國手，體育神經非常好，各種運動都很厲害，有空一定會運動，顯然他的頭痛和他喜愛運動也沒有關係。

appear（v.）出現、顯露
straightforwardly（adv.）直截了當地
explain（v.）解釋、說明
headache（n.）頭痛

examination（n.）檢查
problem（n.）問題
difficult（adj.）困難
cause（n.）原因、病因
illness（n.）疾病

lot, that look again appeared.

This time, I straightforwardly asked Professor Wu what was going on. He explained to me that for about two years now he would suddenly have a headache. He had gone to all kinds of doctors and had been through every type of examination, but no problem could be found. Professor Wu knew that it would be very difficult to find the cause for his illness, because whenever he went to the hospital he would be feeling fine. So how could a doctor find a cause? I asked him if the headache would awaken him while he was sleeping during the night. He said no. I then asked if he had a headache while exercising. He said he didn't seem to. Professor Wu had been a Little League baseball champion, and was quite accomplished in sports. He excelled in every sport and would exercise whenever he had free time. It

---

whenever（conj.）不論何時、每當   baseball（n.）棒球
hospital（n.）醫院   champion（n.）冠軍
awaken（v.）叫醒、喚醒   accomplished（adj.）熟練
exercise（v.）運動、健身   excel（v.）擅長、精通
league（n.）聯盟

　　我決定幫助吳教授解這個謎。我給吳教授一個小小的錄音機，叫他白天用這隨身帶著的錄音機，一旦頭痛就對著錄音機將當時周遭的情形描述一下。我請吳教授將這些頭痛的情況剪輯一下交給我，由我來分析。

　　三個月以後，吳教授給了我一卷錄音帶。我一聽再聽，終於發現了吳教授每次頭痛以前，的確有人做了一件事。這是一件非常普通的事，別人根本無所謂的，但吳教授似乎對這件事非常敏感；當然他自己並不知道他有如此的敏感。

---

obvious（adj.）明顯、顯然
relationship（n.）關係
beloved（adj.）熱愛的、鍾愛的
solve（v.）解決、解答
puzzle（n.）謎、難題
tape（n.）錄音帶

recorder（n.）錄音機
carry（v.）攜帶
as soon as 一…就
pain（n.）疼痛、痛苦
describe（v.）描述、形容
surroundings（n.）環境、周遭事物

was obvious that his headache should have no relationship with his beloved sports.

I decided to help Professor Wu solve this puzzle. I gave him a little tape recorder and asked him to carry it with him during the day. As soon as he had pain in his head, he should use the tape recorder and describe his surroundings. I asked him then to collect and edit his recordings and give them to me. I would analyze them.

Three months later, Professor Wu gave me a tape. I listened to the tape again and again, and discovered that each time before he had the pain, indeed someone had done something. And this was something very ordinary. For other people, this was nothing of any consequence, but Professor Wu was very sensitive to this thing. Of

---

collect（v.）收集
edit（v.）剪輯、編輯
recording（n.）錄音、記錄
analyze（v.）分析
listen to（v.）聆聽
again and again 一再、反覆

discover（v.）發現
indeed（adv.）的確、確實
ordinary（adj.）普通、一般
consequence（n.）重要性
sensitive（adj.）敏感
of course 當然

我決定再對吳教授做進一步的研究。我知道吳教授

這個頭痛的毛病是最近兩年的事，而吳教授在我們學校

裡服務就只有這兩年，而我又注意到吳教授來本校教書

以前，曾經在非洲的一個難民營整整地服務了一年，只

是吳教授好像很少和我們談到他在非洲服務的經驗。

我知道吳教授有記日記的習慣，他在非洲難民營服

務，一定會記日記，所以我向他索取他在那裡記的日

記，他猶豫了一下，後來還是給了我。我拿到日記以

後，開始仔細地看，終於看出了一些端倪。現在輪到我

---

aware of 意識到、知道
sensitivity（n.）敏感
in this regard 關於這件事
follow-up（n.）後續行動
investigation（n.）研究、調查

occur（v.）發生、出現
moreover（adv.）並且、此外
refugee camp（n.）難民營
rare（adj.）很少、罕見
experience（n.）經驗、經歷

course he was not aware of his sensitivity in this regard.

I decided to do a follow-up on my investigation. I knew that his headache was a problem that had occurred during the last two years. Moreover, it was only in the last two years that Professor Wu was working in our school. I also knew that before coming to our school to teach, he had worked at a refugee camp in Africa. But it was rare for him to speak to us about his experiences in Africa.

I also knew that Professor Wu had the habit of keeping a diary, so there should be a diary from when he was at the refugee camp. I asked him if I could get that diary; he was hesitant at first, but eventually gave it to me. After I got the diary, I started to read it carefully. At last I could make sense of his situation. Now it was my

habit（n.）習慣
keep a diary 寫日記
hesitant（adj.）猶豫、遲疑
at first 起先、最初
eventually（adv.）最後、終於

carefully（adv.）小心地、仔細地
at last 最後、終於
make sense of 理解、弄懂
situation（n.）處境、情況

來對症下藥了。

有一天，我和吳教授都要到國科會去開會，回來的時候，吳教授在車上睡著了，我悄悄地將車子開到一家孤兒院去。我對這家孤兒院很熟，這裡有一個三歲大的小男孩，極為可愛，喜歡叫人家抱他。我每次去，他一定會要我抱。我一下車，他就衝了過來，叫我抱他。我抱起了他，他又發現了吳教授，吳教授年輕而又可愛可親，這個小鬼立刻見異思遷，伸出雙手要吳教授抱。而吳教授忽然緊張起來了，似乎很想逃避，但是旁邊很多人看著他，他只好勉為其難地抱起了這個可愛的小孩。

---

medicine（n.）藥
National Science Council（n.）國科會
meeting（n.）會議
fall asleep 睡著

unbeknownst to 不為某人所知
orphanage（n.）孤兒院
familiar（adj.）熟悉
cute（adj.）可愛
hug（v.）擁抱

turn to find him the right medicine for his illness.

One day Professor Wu and I went to the National Science Council for a meeting. Driving back, I saw that he had fallen asleep. I then unbeknownst to him drove to an orphanage with which I was very familiar. There was a three-year-old boy there who was very cute and who loved to be hugged. Every time I went there, he wanted me to hug him. As soon as I got out of the car, he ran over to be hugged. As I was hugging him, he noticed Professor Wu, who was both young and lovable. The little devil, seeing another possibility, changed his mind and extended his hands so as to be hugged by Professor Wu. But Professor Wu all of a sudden became very nervous and it seemed he did not want to do this. But there were many people looking at him, so he had to overcome his hesitancy and hug this cute little child.

---

notice（v.）注意、發現
lovable（adj.）可愛、討人喜歡
devil（n.）魔鬼、傢伙
possibility（n.）可能、合適的人
mind（n.）心意、想法

extend（v.）伸出
all of a sudden 突然、忽然
nervous（adj.）緊張
overcome（v.）克服
hesitancy（n.）猶豫、遲疑

　　小男孩並沒有覺察到吳教授的表情，他緊緊地抱住吳教授，將他的頭靠在吳教授的肩膀上，一副舒適而滿足的模樣。

　　吳教授的緊張表情慢慢地消失了，他抱著孩子離開了我，我注意到他拿下了他的眼鏡，我知道什麼原因，他的淚水流了出來。在回程，吳教授沒有多講話，他好像在回憶一些事，但他也顯得很平靜。

　　我介紹吳教授到一個中途之家去做義工，那裡有一些曾經誤入歧途的青少年，這些年輕人當然崇拜吳教

---

tightly（adv.）緊緊地　　　　　nervousness（n.）緊張
place（v.）放置、安置　　　　　slowly（adv.）慢慢地
shoulder（n.）肩膀　　　　　　disappear（v.）消失
relaxed（adj.）放鬆、閒適　　　move away 離開
satisfied（adj.）滿足、滿意　　take off 拿下、脫下
fashion（n.）模樣、方式

The little boy did not experience Professor Wu's uncomfortableness, and tightly hugged him, placing his head near Professor Wu's shoulders in a most relaxed and satisfied fashion.

The nervousness of Professor Wu slowly disappeared; and he moved away from me while hugging the child. I noticed that he took off his glasses, and I knew the reason why: tears were pouring forth. As we drove back, Professor Wu did not have much to say and seemed to be recalling something, yet he appeared to be very peaceful.

Later on, I introduced Professor Wu to do volunteer work at a half-way house, which had some youngsters who had gotten on the wrong track. These young

---

pour forth 流出
recall（v.）回憶、想起
appear to 似乎、好像
peaceful（adj.）平靜、安詳
later on 後來

introduce（v.）介紹、引介
volunteer（n.）義工
half-way house（n.）中途之家
youngster（n.）青少年
track（n.）軌道、道路

授，他學問好，又會打棒球，游泳也游得好，所以一夜之間，吳教授成了他們的偶像，有什麼問題，都會告訴吳教授。吳教授知道自己並非輔導專家，並不亂給意見，但他至少讓這些孩子們有一個訴說內心話的管道。

吳教授仍然帶著那個錄音機，又三個月過去，他來告訴我他要交白卷了，因為他已不知頭痛為何物矣。

當初我聽吳教授錄音帶的時候，我發現每次吳教授頭痛以前，都曾有人咳嗽過，雖然是很輕微的咳嗽，但是吳教授仍然聽到了；他只要一聽到咳嗽的聲音，就會

---

worship（v.）崇拜、敬仰
well-educated（adj.）學問好、受過
良好教育
swimmer（n.）游泳者
overnight（adv.）一夜之間

hero（n.）英雄、偶像
expert（n.）專家
counseling（n.）輔導、諮詢、諮商
respond（v.）回答、答覆
recklessly（adv.）不顧後果地、魯

people worshipped Professor Wu: he was well-educated and could also play baseball. And. he was a good swimmer, too. Overnight, he became their hero. If they had any problems, they would tell him. Professor Wu knew he was no expert in counseling, so he didn't respond recklessly, but at least he provided a channel for these youngsters to talk from their heart.

Professor Wu continued to carry his tape recorder. After another three months, he came and told me that he was going to give me an empty tape because he no longer knew what a headache was.

Originally, when I had heard Professor Wu's tape, I discovered that each time before he had a headache, there had been someone coughing. Even though it was a very light cough, he had still heard it. He only had to

---

莽地、冒然　　　　　　　　no longer 不再
at least 至少　　　　　　　originally（adv.）起初
provide（v.）提供　　　　　cough（v./n.）咳嗽
channel（n.）管道　　　　　light（adj.）輕微
empty（adj.）空的、空白

感到頭痛。我回想我們上次開會，院長大人訓話的時候，的確曾經咳嗽了一下，我事後還做了一次實驗，我在吳教授附近偷偷地咳嗽一下，他果真又頭痛起來。

為什麼吳教授會對咳嗽如此敏感呢？我知道吳教授曾去過非洲，果真在他的日記中，發現了一段可怕的經驗：他照顧的一個難民小男孩，病死在他的懷中，臨死以前，這個小男孩不停地咳嗽。吳教授的日記中清楚地記錄了這件事。我注意到，吳教授非洲之行的日記到此事件為止，以後就不再記了，可見吳教授心靈受創傷的嚴重性。

---

sermonize（v.）說教、訓話
experiment（n.）實驗
surreptitiously（adv.）偷偷、暗中
expect（v.）預期
mention（v.）提到、提及

unexpectedly（adv.）竟然、意外地
terrifying（adj.）可怕的
look after 照顧、照料
uncontrollably（adv.）無法控制地

hear the sound of coughing to experience the pain. I then remembered that the time when we were at a meeting and our great Dean was sermonizing, our Dean indeed did cough once. Afterwards I did an experiment. When I was near Professor Wu, I surreptitiously coughed, and as to be expected he had a headache.

Why was it that he was so sensitive to a cough? As already mentioned, I knew that Professor Wu had been to Africa. Unexpectedly, in his diary that he had allowed me to read, I discovered a terrifying experience. He had looked after a refugee boy who had died in his arms. Before his death, that little boy had coughed uncontrollably. Professor Wu had recorded this event in his diary very clearly. I further noticed that this brought the diary of his stay in Africa to an end. Afterwards, he wrote no more. Clearly Professor Wu had suffered a very serious psychological wound.

event（n.）事件、事情
clearly（adv.）清楚地、明確地
no more 不再
clearly（adv.）顯然、無疑

suffer（v.）受苦
serious（adj.）嚴重
psychological（adj.）心理的
wound（n.）創傷、受傷

　　吳教授在大學裡一直是幼幼社的社員，也一直喜歡小孩子，這次事件以後，吳教授怕看到小孩，也就不再做義工。但他這種逃避做好事的態度卻使他良心更加不安，反而使他對咳嗽敏感。那個可愛小男孩抱他，使他忽然感到照顧小孩子多麼令他高興，他重回做義工的生涯，也使他知道他仍是個好人，不再對咳嗽敏感了。

　　吳教授告訴我，那天早上去上班，那位病重的小男孩在臨死以前，要他抱，當時這個小男孩已是骨瘦如柴，但沒有想到他居然會緊緊地抱住吳教授達兩個小時之久，小男孩的咳嗽越來越輕，抱的力氣也越來越弱。

---

member（n.）成員、社員　　　　guilty（adj.）內疚的、有罪惡感的
be afraid to 害怕　　　　　　　conscience（n.）良心
escape（v.）逃避、逃跑　　　　return（v.）重返、重回
　　　　　　　　　　　　　　　realize（v.）了解、領悟

At the university, Professor Wu had all along been a member of the Kids Club and had really enjoyed being with kids. After his African experience, he was afraid to be with kids and did not continue this volunteer work. But his trying to escape from doing good work only made him have a guilty conscience, and, even more, made him sensitive to a cough. When that cute little kid hugged him, he suddenly experienced again how happy he was looking after youngsters. And so he returned to his life of doing volunteer work, and made himself realize that he was still a good person. He was no longer sensitive to a cough.

Professor Wu later told me that when he went to work that morning in Africa, the seriously ill boy, before he passed away, had wanted to Professor Wu to hug him. The boy was already as thin as a stick. Professor Wu had had no idea that the boy would want to hug him tightly for two hours. His cough became fainter and

---

seriously（adv.）嚴重
ill（adj.）生病的
pass away 去世、死亡
thin（adj.）瘦弱的

stick（n.）棍、棒
faint（adj.）虛弱的
fainter and faineter 越來越弱

等到他離開人世，吳教授已經快完全崩潰了。

他問我，「如果有人在臨死以前，緊緊地抱著你，你吃得消嗎？」

吳教授又告訴我，自從那個小男孩緊緊地抱住他而又死去以後，他就不再敢抱小孩子，連他姊姊的孩子他也不敢抱。家人都覺得他怪怪地，但不懂他為何如此。他自己也覺得他好可憐，看到可愛的小孩子，竟然不敢去抱。

吳教授說他有一種慾望，那就是幫助別人。他在大

---

strength（n.）力量、力氣
weak（adj.）虛弱的
weaker and weaker越來越弱

completely（adv.）完全、徹底
collapse（v.）崩潰
endure（v.）忍受、吃得消

fainter; the strength of his hugging weaker and weaker. By the time the boy had left this world, Professor Wu had already completely collapsed.

Professor Wu asked me, "If someone, before he died, was tightly hugging you, could you endure it?"

He also told me that since that little boy had died while holding him tightly, he had never again dared to hug a child. Even his sister's children, he did not dare hug. His family members thought he was acting strangely, but they did not understand why. He himself thought he was pitiful since when he saw a lovable child, he did not dare hug him.

Professor Wu also told me that he had one desire:

---

dare（v.）敢
act（v.）行動、表現
strangely（adv.）奇怪地、怪異地

pitiful（adj.）可憐、可悲
desire（n.）慾望

學裡，一直活得很充實，並不是因為他會打球，能考上大學，而是因為他參加了各種服務性的社團，使他的這種慾望得到滿足。非洲之行，使他不敢再做義工，他說他簡直變成了一個禁慾主義者，也就是這樣的禁慾，使他感到十分的痛苦。因為他認為他自己不做好事，不是個好人，這種不做好事的罪惡感使他對咳嗽非常敏感。

吳教授在孤兒院裡抱起小男孩以後，重新感到愛人的快樂，決定又回去做義工，這下他發現他不是個壞人，他仍是個很願意幫助別人的人，他的助人慾望終於得到滿足，頭痛也沒有了。

---

full life 充實
participate（v.）參加、參與
service-related（adj.）服務性質、

與服務有關的
allow（v.）讓、允許
fulfilled（adj.）滿足、實現、完成

to help others. When he was in college, he had a very full life all the time. It was not because he was able to enter college because he could play sports, but it was because he participated in all kinds of service-related clubs, which allowed his desire to help to be fulfilled. His trip to Africa brought to an end his volunteer work. He said that he became someone whose desire was repressed; and it was this kind of repression that made him feel so terribly pained. It was because he thought that he was not doing anything good himself and was not a good person that this guilt of not doing any good things made him so sensitive to a cough.

After Professor Wu had held the little boy in the orphanage, he once again experienced the happiness of loving another person, and decided to return to volunteer work. At that moment he discovered that he was not a bad person. He still was a person who wanted to help others; and his desire to do so was finally again fulfilled.

---

repressed（adj.）抑制的、壓抑的　　guilt（n.）罪惡感
repression（n.）抑制、壓抑　　　　happiness（n.）快樂、幸福
terribly（adv.）很、非常

　　我聽了吳教授的慾望理論以後，發現有那種慾望的人絕對不止他一個人。如果有人禁止我去替小朋友補習，禁止我去探訪病人和受刑人，不准我去安慰沒有考上大學的中學生，也禁止我去抱小孩子，那我就慘了。

　　上個週末，我在孤兒院做義工，那個可愛小男孩又纏著我鬧，我正在想法子將他弄給別人去，來了五位大學生，這五個男生是送錢來的，他們看見了這個小男孩，每個人都想抱他，這個小鬼對這五位大男生端詳一番以後，選了其中一位。那個大男生顯出一臉快樂的表

---

theory（n.）理論
homework（n.）功課、家庭作業
jail（n.）監獄
permit（v.）允許、准許

comfort（v.）安慰
pass（v.）通過
entrance examination（n.）入學考試

There was no more headache.

After I heard Professor Wu's theory of desire, I realized that a person with that kind of desire was not only he himself. If someone would stop me from helping children with their homework, stop me from visiting sick people or people in jail, would not permit me to comfort high school students who had not passed the entrance examination for college, or even would stop me from holding a child, my life too would be miserable.

Last week, when I was doing volunteer work at the orphanage, that loveable boy was making a scene while hanging on to me. As I was thinking how to get him to go to someone else, five male college students appeared who had come to bring some donations. When they saw this boy, they each wanted to hug him. After the little devil sized up the five of them, he selected one. That big

---

miserable（adj.）不幸的、悲慘的　　donation（n.）捐獻、捐贈
make a scene 吵鬧　　　　　　　　size up 打量、端詳
hang on 緊抓不放、黏著（某人）　select（v.）選擇、挑選
male（n.）男子

情，其他的幾位難掩失望之情。

　　我們常常以為慾望不是好事，我們常聽到老師叫學生克制自己的慾望。但吳教授說得對，我們都有一種潛在的慾望，想去愛人，想去關懷別人，也想去做些善事。我們這種慾望，如果不能得到滿足，是不會快樂的。吳教授就是一個很好的例子。

　　　　　　　　──原載八十九年六月二十五日《聯合副刊》

express（v.）顯露、表現出
conceal（v.）隱藏、掩蓋
disappointment（n.）失望、沮喪

frequently（adv.）經常、屢屢
control（v.）控制、克制

college student expressed his happiness, and the others could not conceal their disappointment.

We often think that desire is not something good, and frequently hear teachers tell students to control their desires. Professor Wu, however, is right. We all have a subconscious desire to love others, to be concerned about others, and to do something good. If this desire cannot be fulfilled, we will not be happy. Professor Wu is such a good example.

---

subconscious（adj.）潛在的、潛意
識的

concern（v.）關心、關懷
example（n.）例子、範例

譯者簡介

康士林（Nicholas Koss）

美國印第安那大學比較文學博士，現任天主教輔仁大學比較文學研究所所長。自一九八一年起於輔仁大學英國文學系任教迄今。康教授並於輔仁大學比較文學研究所與翻譯學研究所授課。最近剛卸下六年任期的外語學院院長行政職。康教授著作有：專書 *The Best and Fairest Land: Medieval Images of China*（台北 1999），數篇比較文學相關學術論文及台灣 *The Chinese Pen* 翻譯文章，譯有《跟李伯伯學英文1：*Page* 21》一書。

鮑端磊（Daniel J. Bauer）

美國威斯康辛比較文學博士。天主教神父，現為天主教輔仁大學英國語文學系副教授兼進修部英文系主任。近年來，英譯的中文短篇故事，散見於 *The Chinese Pen*、*The Free China Review* 及 *Inter-religio*（香港）等期刊。譯有《跟李伯伯學英文1：*Page* 21》一書。自一九九五年九月以來，即每星期為英文中國郵報（*The China Post*）撰寫專欄，討論有關教育及社會議題。目前在輔仁大學英國語文學系所開設的課程有翻譯、十八世紀英國文學、二十世紀初美國文學等。

校訂者簡介

強勇傑

國立台灣大學外國語文學系所畢業，現為國立台灣師範大學翻譯研究所博士生。擔任中華民國筆會中英校訂多年。八十九年獲第十三屆梁實秋文學獎短篇小說中譯英優選，九十年獲第一屆文建會文學翻譯獎譯詩組中譯英佳作，九十一年獲第十五屆梁實秋文學獎譯文組英譯中優等獎；九十二年獲第二屆文建會文學翻譯獎譯文組中譯英佳作。

九歌譯叢最新叢書

F0924	法國文化教室	翁德明 編	定價230元
	——跨越時空的法國文化之旅		
F0923	世界情詩名作100首	陳黎・張芬齡 譯	定價250元
F0922	綠色奇蹟——辻原登小說集	辻原登 著／林水福 譯	定價180元
F0920	真愛永不敗北	莎岡 著／胡品清 譯	定價190元
F0918	自言自語——美語錄第三集	喬志高 著	定價240元
F0917	聽其言也——美語錄第二集	喬志高 著	定價240元
F0916	言猶在耳——美語錄第一集	喬志高 著	定價230元
F0915	星闌干	井上靖 著／喬遷 譯	
			定價平裝260元・精裝380元
F0914	荒鷲武士	板井三郎 著／黃文範 譯	
			定價280元
F0913	西洋文學大教室	彭鏡禧 主編	定價300元
	——精讀經典		
F0910	拒絕出生的胎兒	巴斯卡・卡內克律 著／李雪玲 譯	
			定價200元
F0909	乾河道	井上靖 著／喬遷 譯	
			定價平裝220元・精裝360元
F0908	震驚世界的那一夜	華特勞德 著／黃文範 譯	
	——鐵達尼沉沒記		定價190元
F0907	我沒有時間了	金曉蕾・張香華 譯	定價250元
	——南斯拉夫詩選		
F0906	拿破崙愛與死	拿破崙 著／徐梅芬 譯	定價250元

F0905 喬伊斯傳　　　　　　　　　　彼得・寇斯提羅 著／林玉珍 譯
　　──愛爾蘭時期的愛情與文學　　　　　　　　　定價320元

F0904 尤利西斯（下）　　　　　　　喬伊斯 著／金隄 譯
　　　　　　　　　　　　　　　　　定價平裝650元・精裝750元

F0903 尤利西斯（上）　　　　　　　喬伊斯 著／金隄 譯
　　　　　　　　　　　　　　　　　定價平裝650元・精裝750元

F0902 杜連魁　　　　　　　　　　　王爾德 著／王大閎 譯　定價250元

F0901 我兒子的故事　　　　　　　　娜汀・葛蒂瑪 著／彭淮棟 譯
　　　　　　　　　　　　　　　　　　　　　　　　定價190元

◎ 上列作品單冊八五折。團體購書，另有優待，請電洽。
◎ 日後定價如有變動，請以各該書新版定價為準。
◎ 購書方法：
　　・網路訂購：九歌文學網：www.chiuko.com.tw
　　・郵政劃撥：01122951，九歌出版社有限公司
　　・信用卡購書單，電索即傳。請回傳：02-2578-9205
　　・電洽客服部：02-2577-6564 分機9

版權所有　翻印必究

九歌譯叢 ⑨36

跟李伯伯學英文2：Good Fate（有聲書）

著　　　者：李　家　同
譯　　　者：鮑　端　磊、康　士　林
校　　　訂：強　勇　傑
責 任 編 輯：何　靜　婷
發 行 人：蔡　文　甫
發 行 所：九歌出版社有限公司
　　　　　　臺北市八德路3段12巷57弄40號
　　　　　　電話／02-25776564・傳眞／02-25789205
　　　　　　郵政劃撥／0112295-1
九歌文學網：www.chiuko.com.tw
登 記 證：行政院新聞局局版臺業字第1738號
印 刷 所：晨捷印製股份有限公司
法 律 顧 問：龍躍天律師・蕭雄淋律師・董安丹律師
初　　　版：2009（民國98）年08月10日

定　價：280元

ISBN 978-957-444-610-0　　　　　　Printed in Taiwan

書號：F0936

（缺頁、破損或裝訂錯誤，請寄回本公司更換）

國家圖書館出版品預行編目資料

跟李伯伯學英文.2, Good Fate／李家同著；
康士林，鮑端磊譯. — 初版. —臺北市：
九歌，民98.08
　面； 公分. —（九歌譯叢；936）
中英對照
ISBN　978-957-444-610-0　　　（平裝）

1.英語　2.讀本

805.18　　　　　　　　　　98011184